# The Ghost of Lunenburg Manor

**THE TOM AUSTEN MYSTERIES**
by Eric Wilson

Terror in Winnipeg
Murder on *The Canadian*
Vancouver Nightmare
The Lost Treasure of Casa Loma
Disneyland Hostage
The Kootenay Kidnapper
Vampires of Ottawa
Spirit in the Rainforest
The Green Gables Detectives

A TOM & LIZ AUSTEN MYSTERY

# The Ghost of Lunenburg Manor

## ERIC WILSON

Stoddart

First published in hardcover in 1981 by Clarke, Irwin & Company Limited
First published in paperback in 1982 by Totem Books,
a division of Collins Publishers
Published in 1993 by Stoddart Publishing Co. Limited

Published in Canada in 2000 by
Stoddart Kids,
a division of Stoddart Publishing Co. Limited
895 Don Mills Road, 400–2 Centre Place
Toronto, Canada M3C 1W3
Tel (416) 445-3333 Fax (416) 445-5967
E-mail cservice@genpub.com

Published in the United States in 2000 by
Stoddart Kids,
a division of Stoddart Publishing Co. Limited
180 Varick Street, 9th Floor
New York, New York 10014
Toll free 1-800-805-1083
E-mail gdsinc@genpub.com

Distributed in Canada by
General Distribution Services
325 Humber College Blvd.
Toronto, Canada M9W 7C3
Tel (416) 213-1919 Fax (416) 213-1917
E-mail cservice@genpub.com

Distributed in the United States by
General Distribution Services, PMB 128
4500 Witmer Industrial Estates
Niagara Falls, New York 14305–1386
Toll free 1-800-805-1083
E-mail gdsinc@genpub.com

04 03 02 01 00 5 6 7 8 9

**Canadian Cataloguing in Publication Data**

Wilson, Eric
The ghost of Lunenburg manor

ISBN: 0-7736-7484-5

I. Title.

PS8595.I583G56 1999    jC813'.54    C99-931324-X
PZ7.W54Gh 1999

Cover Design: Brant Cowie/ArtPlus
Cover Illustration: Jane Lawrason

*We acknowledge for their financial support of our publishing program the
Government of Canada through the Book Publishing Industry Development
Program (BPIDP), the Canada Council, and the Ontario Arts Council.*

*This book is dedicated to*
*Terry Fox*
*And to the memory of my father*
*R.S.S. Wilson*
*Courageous fighters*
*against a common enemy*

# 1

"It's the ghost of the *Young Teazer*!"

The old fisherman pointed a trembling finger at the fire across the sea. "It's come back, to haunt us all."

A group of people stood on the wharf, gazing through the darkness at the blazing light. The only sound came from waves washing against the rocky shore.

A light wind carried the salty sea air to Tom Austen, a red-headed boy with many freckles, and his slim, dark-haired sister, Liz. "Who's this guy Teazer?" she asked the fisherman.

"It's a ship, not a person. During the War of 1812 the *Young Teazer* was trapped here by the British navy. One of the men, knowing he was doomed to swing from an English yardarm, deliberately blew up his own vessel. They say it was terrible, how the sky exploded into flames and the crewmen screamed as they died."

"But how can we be seeing the same ship?"

"That's the strange thing. Exactly a year after it blew up, the *Young Teazer* came back as a ghost ship. People saw a ball of fire sail across this bay, then suddenly flare up in a silent explosion and disappear. Since then, many have told of seeing the *Teazer* light."

Tom gasped in surprise. "It's gone! Did you see how it just vanished?"

The fisherman nodded. "I'll be going home. We won't see the ghost ship again this night."

The old man turned away, and most of the others followed. As they left, their faces were briefly lit by the headlights of a car that came speeding out of the night.

"Here's Professor Zinck," said one of the people who remained, "but he's too late."

A man with a large oval stomach and a large oval face came quickly along the wharf. Besides a nose of remarkable size, his face included heavy glasses and a goatee bristling with short, black hairs.

"Have I missed it?"

"Yes, and it's a shame. You could have written

2

about the ghost ship in your next book, Professor."

"Please tell me what happened."

After hearing several descriptions, Professor Zinck shook his head. "I'm sorry I missed it. The light may have been a prank, but I can't say for sure."

Tom looked up at the big man. "If you're going to investigate, sir, my sister and I would like to help."

But before the Professor could reply, a pretty woman with greying hair stepped forward. "Now, Tom, there's to be no detective work. Your parents want you to have a nice, relaxing holiday."

Professor Zinck gave her a puzzled look. "What's this all about, Shirley?"

Smiling, she introduced Tom and Liz. "Their parents have sent these two to my guest house for a holiday. They thought a fishing village like Stonehurst would be perfect, because Tom and Liz couldn't get mixed up in any mysteries."

The Professor chuckled. "There are lots of mysteries and strange events in Nova Scotia, but I guess I'd better not mention any."

Liz gave him an encouraging smile. "Won't you tell us just one, Professor? I'm sure that won't hurt."

Shirley gave Professor Zinck a warning look, but he chuckled again and pretended not to notice. "Would you two like to visit a haunted house?"

"Wow! You bet!"

Shirley shook her head. "I don't think . . ."

3

Professor Zinck laughed. "Now then, Shirley, these kids can't come to harm in my own home."

Tom stared at him in amazement. "You mean you *live* in a haunted house?"

The Professor nodded. "Come and meet my wife. She's actually seen the Lady in White who haunts Lunenburg Manor, where we live. Perhaps you'd join us for supper tomorrow, and Annette can tell you her story."

They walked along the wharf past piles of nets and the powerful smells of fish and salt, and stopped beside an expensive car. In the driver's seat was a woman who had hair and eyes as black as the Professor's. Smiling warmly, she agreed to tell them about the Lady in White the next evening.

"Are you frightened of ghosts?"

"I'm not," Tom said, "but my sister is scared of vampires."

"That's a lie!" Liz protested.

"Well, you're superstitious. That's practically the same thing."

"It is not!"

Mrs. Zinck smiled at Liz. "If you want superstitions, Nova Scotia is the place to be. I've known hundreds since I was a child."

Liz grinned, and turned to Shirley. "I've heard some great ones here. Like this morning, when Wade started singing at the table."

"That boy!" Shirley said. "I know he did it to tease me, but now someone's life is threatened."

Liz nodded. "Sing at the table, sing at a funeral. That's what the superstition says."

"Brrrr," Shirley said, rubbing her hands ner-

4

vously. "Let's all go to my place for coffee, and forget about singing at funerals."

Everyone piled into the car for the short ride to "The Fisherman's Home," which was the name of Shirley's guest house. As they drove, Tom looked at Professor Zinck.

"What kind of books have you written?"

"Collections of ghost stories and superstitions, tales of buried treasure and shipwrecks. I love writing about the Maritimes because everyone here has a story to tell."

"Did you say *buried treasure*?"

"That's right. Pirates used to put into Nova Scotia before heading for Europe. Pieces of eight and other treasures have been dug up, and some say that Captain Kidd's wealth may be buried at the bottom of Oak Island's Money Pit."

"I've heard of Oak Island," Liz said. "Isn't it near here?"

He nodded. "Why don't we visit the Money Pit together on Tuesday? I don't know if Kidd's gold is actually down there, but it's still a bizarre place to see."

"That would be great!"

Bright lights shone from the windows of "The Fisherman's Home" as Mrs. Zinck parked the car. Everyone walked toward the front door except Shirley and Liz, who disappeared around the corner of the house.

"Brother!" Tom said. "Liz is getting impossible."

"Where have they gone?"

"When we left for the wharf earlier tonight, we went out the back door. So Shirley and Liz are

5

going in by the same door, to avoid bad luck."

"Maybe you should too," Mrs. Zinck suggested.

"I'm not superstitious!" Pulling open the front door, Tom stepped inside and turned to Mrs. Zinck. "You see? The ceiling didn't fall on my head."

"That's not how superstitions work, Tom. Let's just hope you haven't jinxed yourself, or someone else."

"No way." Tossing his jacket at a chair, Tom went into the living room where two men were reading. One was Shirley's husband, Carl Goulden, who stood up to greet the Zincks, and the other was a paying guest named Roger Eliot-Stanton. Tall and bony, he had refused to answer any of Tom's questions and often spent long hours locked in his room.

"Hey, Mr. Eliot-Stanton!" Tom exclaimed. "You should have seen the ghost ship! The sky exploded into flames, and you could almost hear the screams of the dying crewmen!"

Lamplight shadowed the deep hollows of Roger Eliot-Stanton's face as he looked up from his book. "There are no ghosts," he said, and then left the room just as Liz walked in.

"What a party-pooper that guy is," she said. "Maybe it's his funeral we'll be singing at."

When Carl had finished making the coffee, he smiled at Professor Zinck. "Would you work the ouija board with us?"

"A ouija board!" Liz jumped up from her chair. "May I try it? Please, Carl! I'm sure I can summon spirits."

"I don't know, Liz."

"Please! What's wrong with a ouija board?"

Carl smiled. "O.K., you can give it a try."

As he lit some candles, Shirley went to get their children, Carla, Holli and Todd. "A big group helps summon the spirits," she explained. "Luckily Wade isn't here, or he'd make fun of us all."

Liz sat down at the ouija board, opposite Shirley. "Spirit of the past," Shirley chanted, "are you with us? Answer yes."

All eyes watched the board in the yellow candlelight. Somewhere in the house a clock ticked, and Tom was aware of the wind sighing through the trees, but there was no other sound. Seconds passed into minutes and then, with a terrible crash, the outside door flew open.

Shouts and screams were heard, then someone reached for the light switch. In the doorway stood the Gouldens' teenaged son, Wade, his face shining with sweat.

"Hey, everyone!" he said in an excited voice. "I just heard about the ghost ship! I ran all the way to the wharf, but it was gone. What was it like?"

Carl gave him an irritated look. "You've just scared everyone half to death, Wade."

"Sorry, Dad. Say, is it true you saw the ghost of the *Young Teazer*?"

"It's possible."

Wade grinned at Tom. "Hey, man, I'm surprised to see you sitting around. Why haven't you started your investigation of the *Teazer* light?"

"There are no ghosts," Tom said, trying to sound as haughty as Roger Eliot-Stanton.

Professor Zinck finished his coffee with a quick swallow. "It's getting late, my dear," he said to his wife.

She smiled at Tom and Liz. "I'll look forward to telling you about the Lady in White. My husband doesn't drive, so I'll pick you up tomorrow."

"Thanks, Mrs. Zinck. We can't wait to see your haunted house!"

After helping to clean up the kitchen, Tom went to his bedroom in the back of the house. For a while he sat at the open window, listening to the wind sweeping through the woods, then got into bed and lay with his eyes on the dark ceiling.

What was the mysterious light out at sea? If it really *was* a ghost ship, had it appeared as a warning to beware of strangers? As for strangers, why had Professor Zinck been so quick to invite Tom and Liz to visit his haunted house, and even take them to Oak Island? Maybe an ancient curse hung over Lunenburg Manor, a curse that required the sacrifice of young blood.

Sighing deeply, Tom rolled over in bed. They'd been fools to accept an invitation from a stranger who could secretly be *anything*, even a vampire. With a shudder, he pictured the Zincks in the doorway of Lunenburg Manor, fangs glistening and black capes swirling as werewolves howled somewhere in the night.

Tom sighed again, and tried to think of a happier subject. As he began to drift into sleep, images of ghost ships and vampires loomed in his mind. Then, without warning, he felt icy fingers touch his neck.

# 2

Tom's eyes flew open.

His teeth chattering, he stared at his pillow in terror, waiting for the next touch of those ice-cold fingers. When nothing happened, he leapt from the bed with clenched fists, ready to fight.

The room was empty and still. Warm night air billowed the curtains, but nothing else moved as Tom waited for his heart to return to normal. Finally he got back into bed, but it was a long time before he fell asleep.

The next day Tom didn't mention the icy fingers, knowing how happy Liz and Wade would be to repeat the story when things got dull. But he did manage to laugh off his fears about the Zincks being vampires, and felt relaxed that evening as Mrs. Zinck drove them to the nearby community of Lunenburg. Expecting to see just another town, Tom was startled by its unusual beauty.

"What great old houses! Look at the spires on that one!"

Mrs. Zinck smiled. "Lunenburg was founded in 1753 by settlers from Germany, and they brought a distinctive style of architecture with them. Do you see that house's dormer, overhanging the street? That's called a 'bump,' and they say it's a great room for watching what your neighbours are doing!"

"This is fantastic. Like a fairy land," Liz said, staring at a house with gingerbread decorations around its gables. "I love all the flowers, and the bright colours of the houses."

"Look at that one!" Tom exclaimed. "It reminds me of a wedding cake, with all those little roofs piled on top of each other. They could make a great movie in Lunenburg."

Mrs. Zinck laughed. "They already have. In fact, a company wanted to make a horror movie in our house, but we refused."

"A horror movie? How come?"

"I guess because it's old, and the tower makes it look a bit creepy."

They drove past brilliant-red buildings at the harbour, where gillnetters rode at anchor, then climbed a hill into a residential area where the streets were pleasantly shaded by old trees.

"Here's Lunenburg Manor," Mrs. Zinck said, as

she pulled up in front of a large house with peaked windows and towers.

"It *would* make a great horror movie! I'd give anything to live in a house like this!"

"Even with a ghost?"

"Especially with a ghost!"

Tom and Liz got out and stood gazing at the Manor. Something about the menacing dark windows gave Tom the feeling he was being watched, but he just laughed at his nerves.

The porch steps creaked under their feet. Until now Tom had felt light-hearted about visiting a genuine haunted house, but his pulse quickened as he approached the front door with its heavy wood and etched glass. Why couldn't he get rid of the feeling that hidden eyes were watching?

"What's for supper, Mrs. Zinck?"

Liz shot him a look. "Talk about rude!"

"What's wrong with feeling hungry?"

Mrs. Zinck smiled. "I think you'll enjoy the meal, Tom. We're having *kartoffelsuppe* and Solomon Gundy."

The door opened without warning, revealing a thin man with a heavily lined face. "Welcome to Lunenburg Manor," he said, holding out a hand that felt brittle to the touch. "We've been expecting you."

Tom tried to smile, but the man's dusty voice and drooping eyes gave him a chill. Maybe he spent his nights in the cellar, creating the next Frankenstein out of spare parts collected from supper guests.

Tom stepped reluctantly into the hallway. On

11

the wall was a sword, its silver blade reflecting the dying sun. Nearby was a faded picture of a runaway horse with a rider whose eyes goggled in fear.

"The meal will be served in forty-five minutes, madam."

"Thank you, Henneyberry." Mrs. Zinck looked down the shadowy hallway, then went to a mirror and arranged her already perfect black hair. Again she looked at the hallway, then at Henneyberry.

"When are we eating?"

"In forty-five minutes, madam."

"Oh yes, I believe you just told me." For a second time, Mrs. Zinck's hands went to her hair without finding anything to do. "Henneyberry," she said after a pause, "I'd like to see how dinner's coming along."

He nodded his head, and shuffled along the hallway behind Mrs. Zinck. As a door closed silently behind them, Tom looked at Liz.

"Wow! That guy could star as the phantom of the Rue Morgue."

"I think he's kinda cute, with his shiny head and perfectly rounded shoulders."

"What's wrong with Mrs. Zinck? As soon as we came in the door she started acting strange."

"Maybe she's worried about something."

"She's probably scared of Henneyberry. I'll bet she's going to check the soup in case he's spiked it with cyanide."

"Listen, Tom, even if the soup tastes funny, you

12

eat it. Don't do anything gross, like spitting it out, or Mom and Dad will be furious."

"Only if you squeal to them! Try it, and . . ."

Liz raised a warning hand as the door opened and Mrs. Zinck emerged. With a bright smile, she motioned them toward a room where a grandfather clock ticked loudly.

"I'm sorry I kept you waiting."

"Are you O.K., Mrs. Zinck?"

"Of course!"

She cranked up her smile a few more watts, but it still looked unreal to Tom. Thinking about Henneyberry, alone in the kitchen with the soup, made the hairs on his neck tingle.

"Let's sit down, kids, and I'll tell you about the Lady in White."

"At last!"

The room was tastefully furnished with a thick Chinese carpet, red velvet curtains looped beside the tall windows, and elegant white candles in a candelabra above the fireplace.

"Many generations of people have lived in Lunenburg Manor," Mrs. Zinck said. "Two winters ago, I was awakened by the sound of a horse, galloping away into the night. Nothing unusual in that, perhaps, except that we checked the snow in the morning and there were no footprints."

"Could they have drifted in?"

Mrs. Zinck shook her head. "It hadn't snowed overnight. Well, I decided it was all a dream, and had almost forgotten about it when I began hearing hollow knocks in my room. It was a strangely empty sound, and I can tell you it scared me, especially the night when I was awakened by the knocking and then had the covers yanked off my bed."

"Wow! What did you do?"

"I screamed. My husband came running from his room, threw on the lights, and found me shaking with terror. The covers were in a heap on the floor, and I can assure you it wasn't me who'd put them there."

For a second Tom imagined he'd actually heard hollow knocks coming from somewhere above, and his eyes rolled toward the ceiling. "Did either of you just hear a knocking sound?"

Liz laughed. "My brother has a 100-megawatt imagination, Mrs. Zinck. In a few more minutes he'll be screaming down the road."

Tom's face went red. "This house gives me the creeps. It's almost like there's something evil here."

Mrs. Zinck stared at him. "You can feel it, too?"

"I can sure feel something."

For a moment she continued to stare, then turned to Liz. "Zinck is a German name, and both my husband and I are descended from the original settlers of Lunenburg. You may have heard the term *poltergeist*, which comes from the German and means 'playful spirit.' At first we thought such a spirit inhabited the Manor, but later we decided that it must be the ghost of a very sad person."

"What happened?"

"I began to notice the scent of roses, and one night I heard light footsteps in my room. They

14

crossed to the closet, and there was something that sounded like the rustling of a petticoat, but I could see nothing, in spite of the bright moonlight. Then a week later I did see her, after some force had made me go up to the attic."

"*Made* you go up? All by yourself?"

Mrs. Zinck nodded. "A lady in a wedding dress stood by the window. Her head was bowed, and she was crying. I was filled with sadness, and was walking forward to comfort her when she vanished, leaving the room as cold as ice. For some reason I was no longer afraid, now that I'd actually seen the ghost, but I decided I had to learn her story. After doing a lot of research, I found out that a young lady who once lived here had been deeply in love with a man who left her and married another woman. Shortly after, the unhappy girl hanged herself in the attic of the Manor."

"Oh no!"

"They say that some ghosts are the spirits of those who have died tragically, and cannot find peace. I think the Lady in White wanted me to hear the sound of her lover, galloping away on horseback after he'd broken her heart, and then wanted me to learn her story so that someone in the Manor would know of her sadness."

Liz shook her head. "Men make me sick."

Tom's eyebrows rose dramatically. "Is that why your bedroom walls are covered with their pictures?"

"Every night I throw darts at those pictures."

"And every morning you kiss and make up. I've heard your rubbery lips going *smack! smack!*"

15

Mrs. Zinck laughed. "You two remind me of being young. I was always bickering with my brother."

Liz smiled at her. "I'll bet you'd agree that we could end the world's problems by putting all of the men on an Arctic island."

"With Liz in charge!" Tom said. "She'd love it."

The large shape of Professor Zinck appeared in the doorway. "Good evening. Have you heard about the Lady in White?"

Tom nodded. "It's a sad story. I always thought ghosts were things to be scared of, not feel sorry for."

Professor Zinck looked at his wife. "It's almost time to eat, and there's still no sign of our other guest. Should I go up the hill, to see if he's prowling around the graveyard?"

"I don't think that's necessary, dear. Why don't you show Tom and Liz some of the treasures?"

"Good idea." The Professor pressed a button, and Henneyberry materialized in the doorway. "Please bring the leather case from the safe."

"If you wish, sir."

During the long wait for Henneyberry to return, an Irish setter with a gleaming red coat came into the room, sat directly at the Professor's feet, and raised its handsome head for patting. After receiving a generous helping of affection, the dog stretched out and instantly fell asleep. Raucous snoring filled the room, making Tom laugh.

"What's his name?"

"Boscawen, but we call him 'Boss' for short. The name comes from an Admiral in the British navy."

Henneyberry returned, carrying a small leather case. Taking up a position beside the Professor, he watched Tom and Liz with narrowed eyes.

Professor Zinck ran his fingers over the leather case, enjoying its smooth texture, then placed it on a low marble table and snapped open the catches. There was a glint of gold as he took out a coin, and placed it in Liz's hand.

"You're holding a *louis d'or*, my dear. You may rest assured it's worth a pretty penny."

Liz twisted her hand, and the coin disappeared. Henneyberry gasped in shock, then nearly had heart failure as Liz reached up and found the coin behind his ear. The Zincks laughed heartily, and applauded.

"Just a little trick I taught myself," Liz said, bowing. "I'm glad I finally got to try it!"

Tom burned with envy. Not only had Liz secretly learned the coin trick, but she had found the perfect time to use it. "Do you want to see my *numero uno* card trick? It will amaze you!"

"Perhaps later, Tom." Professor Zinck dropped several gold coins in his hand. "These come from the sea bed. It's estimated that five thousand wrecks lie off the Nova Scotia coast. The coins belong to a friend who dives as a hobby, and who recently came up with *this* splendid object from a wreck."

The Professor reached into the case, and lifted out a golden goblet sparkling with jewels. "Rubies

17

and emeralds," he said, pointing to the gorgeous stones. "Amethysts and sapphires."

"It must be worth a fortune!"

"At least."

"Did you say a friend owns this goblet and the coins?" Liz smiled. "If he's single, I wouldn't mind meeting him."

"But Liz," Tom said sarcastically, "wouldn't he make you sick?"

"Some men are exceptions to the rule."

"That's right, I'd forgotten. Liz hates all men, except those between the ages of five and ninety-five."

The Professor glanced toward the doorway, and his face broke into a wide smile. "Well, speak of the devil. Here's the treasure's owner now."

Tom turned, half expecting to see someone handsome in expensive clothes and flashy diamond rings. Instead, he was surprised to see worn jeans and an old denim jacket, a long and lean body, and a face that—with its thick black beard, fierce eyes and deeply creased skin—needed only an eye-patch to become the very picture of a pirate. The man's black eyes flashed straight to the gold coins in Tom's hand, making his heart pound.

"You going to take those home?"

"No, sir."

The savage black eyes studied Tom's face. "Go ahead. Put them in your pocket."

Tom walked nervously to the leather case. The coins clinked as he dropped them in, and he breathed a quiet sigh of relief as he knelt down to rub the Irish setter's head. Who *was* this person?

The Professor returned the goblet to the case, and chuckled as he stood up. "Still trying to give your wealth away, my friend? What an attitude!" Taking the stranger by the arm, he walked toward Liz. "Come and meet a young lady who has some interesting ideas about men."

Blushing, Liz held out her hand. "Hi. I'm Liz Austen."

"I'm Black Dog," the man said.

After introducing Tom, the Professor put his arm around Black Dog's shoulders and gave him a friendly squeeze. "Kids, you are privileged to meet one of Canada's great artists. A neglected genius, who will one day be hailed in the capitals of the world!"

The man looked slightly embarrassed, but didn't deny that he might be a genius. Henneyberry, however, snorted with contempt before closing the leather case and carrying it out of the room.

"Don't drop it," Black Dog called after him.

A mutter came from the hallway as Henneyberry shuffled away. There was an awkward silence, then Black Dog glanced at Tom. "Why didn't you pocket the coins?"

"Because they're yours."

"I don't want the things."

The Professor smiled. Picking up a decanter, he poured richly coloured sherry into crystal glasses which he then handed to his wife and Black Dog. "A libation on the altar of good friendship," he said, lifting his glass.

"Cheers." Black Dog knocked back his drink, and smacked his red lips vigorously. "Always the best sherry. You people live well."

"So could you, Black Dog. Just cash in those coins and the goblet, and you'll be rich. Then you can sculpt full time, rather than sweating your life away in the school's boiler room."

"I like my job. Besides, too much money is an evil thing. I want no part of those treasures, so they're yours for good."

Mrs. Zinck shook her head. "We're only keeping them safe for you, Black Dog. You need lots of money to finance your art, which is why you'll inherit everything we have when we die. Except for some money left to Henneyberry and the Professor's brother, it will all be yours."

Black Dog turned to the Professor, suddenly furious. "I've told you before, leave it *all* to your brother! I refuse it!"

Professor Zinck shook his head sadly. "My friend," he sighed, "when will you come to your senses? You deserve the money, not my brother. He broke my parents' hearts, so they left him nothing. I know they would want their riches to be passed to a young genius like you."

"Rubbish."

Henneyberry's solemn face appeared out of the shadows in the hallway. "The meal is ready."

"Excellent!" The Professor rubbed his big hands in anticipation, then held out his arm and led Mrs. Zinck across the hallway to the dining room. Liz waited hopefully for Black Dog to be as gallant, but he helped himself to another quick sherry and left the room without offering her even a glance.

"Men!"

"Let's eat," Tom said, hurrying across to the dining room. Large and dark, it was lit by chandeliers and orange flames which leapt in a marble fireplace. The Zincks were at opposite ends of a long table set with crystal and silver that reflected the sparkle of candlelight.

"Please sit here, Tom." Above Mrs. Zinck was an unusual oval portrait of a man. One of his eyes looked straight at Tom, the other was focussed on the fireplace. Tom tried to avoid the sinister eye, but there was nothing else to look at except the twisted shadows thrown on the wall by a towering bamboo-palm. Against his will, Tom remembered last night's icy fingers and he felt his neck tingle.

He looked at Mrs. Zinck, trying to laugh. "My nerves are on edge. I guess because this house is haunted."

"Then perhaps I'd better not mention that we also have bats."

"*What*?"

She laughed. "They nest in the attic, and fly around the rooms at night. They're scary, of course, but the patterns they make in flight are really quite beautiful."

The Professor nodded. "They go *tssch-tssch* as they fly, and I'd swear they're laughing at the hopeless attempts Boss makes to catch them. Bats are very useful, you know, because they eat vast numbers of insects."

"That's O.K., but how much blood do they drink every night? I'm too young to be a donor."

"You've been watching too many late-night movies, Tom."

21

Henneyberry grew out of the shadows, which seemed to be his favourite trick. The dancing candlelight made his lined face seem especially long and solemn as he moved slowly around the table, placing a bowl of soup in front of each person.

"*Kartoffelsuppe*," he said in Tom's ear, the muttered word sounding like an ancient curse. "Do enjoy it."

"Thanks," Tom said shakily, then waited for Black Dog to try the soup. When the man had done so—and not fallen to the floor clutching his throat in agony—Tom took a sip and discovered that it was delicious.

"Do you like it?" Mrs. Zinck asked. "The schooner crews often had this soup while fishing out on the Grand Banks."

Professor Zinck snapped his fingers. "I knew I'd forgotten something. Next time the kids visit, we must offer them baked fish tongues as a treat." When Tom and Liz stared silently at each other, he laughed. "Just joking, of course, but the crews used to eat all of the fish: tongues, jowls, hearts. It was the most easily available food, do you see? Plus they enjoyed lots of goodies while out fishing, like apple schnitzel and pumpkin pie."

"Aren't you having any soup, Mrs. Zinck?"

She shook her head. "I must watch my diet very carefully. I'm a diabetic."

"Do you take insulin shots?"

"Yes," she said, then changed the subject. "Ah! Here comes the Solomon Gundy."

This turned out to be small pieces of raw herring, served with onion and a wedge of lemon. After the delicious *kartoffelsuppe*, Tom was disappointed when the herring had very little flavour. His taste buds were soon back in action, however, as Henneyberry produced an excellent haddock covered in crushed almonds and surrounded by slices of fried banana.

"Fantastic!" Liz said, as she polished off her haddock. "I've barely got room for dessert."

Henneyberry made another silent entrance, bearing plates of deep-fried apple segments rolled in cinnamon. Each slice was crisp on the outside, and steaming-hot inside.

"What a feast," Tom said, pushing back his chair and rubbing his swollen belly. "Mr. Henneyberry is a genius cook."

"You're right, Tom," Professor Zinck said, "and we're lucky he's here. An expensive Halifax restaurant tried to lure him away, but we kept him by raising his pay a bit. Not that money seems important to Henneyberry!"

As the Professor laughed, Henneyberry's sad wet eyes watched him from the shadows. Tom felt a surge of pity for the old man, although he couldn't tell why.

"Can we help with the dishes?"

"No thanks, Tom." Mrs. Zinck looked at her watch. "Perhaps I should drive you home now."

"Thanks for the great meal, Mr. Henneyberry."

For the first time that evening, the solemn face smiled. "Please come again."

In the hallway they were putting on their jackets when Tom noticed a bookcase containing a collection of volumes, each with the words *by Professor C. Zinck.* "Hey, neat! Here's all your books."

"What an output," Liz said admiringly. "I have trouble scratching together enough words for a single essay."

"Say, Professor Zinck, what's your first name? Is it something unusual like Caliph or Carim?"

He laughed, "My name certainly is unusual. It's Carol. You see, my parents failed to have the daughters they always wanted, so they stuck their two sons with girls' names."

Smiling, Mrs. Zinck hugged her husband. "I can tell you really like Tom and Liz. Only your closest friends know the truth about your name."

"You're right, my dear! It's been a very pleasant evening, and I'm looking forward to visiting Oak Island tomorrow with the kids."

"Thanks a million, Professor."

After saying goodnight, Tom and Liz went out into the darkness with Mrs. Zinck. Walking toward the car, she suddenly stopped and looked up at the looming black outline of Lunenburg Manor.

"Thank goodness you were here tonight!"

"Why, Mrs. Zinck?"

"Because it took my mind off my fears. Tom, do you remember saying you felt the presence of evil in the Manor?"

"Well, it's not that I was scared or anything, but . . ."

"I've always loved our home, but lately I've been so frightened. I have this terrible feeling that someone is about to suffer a horrible fate in Lunenburg Manor."

# 3

Early the next morning, Tom and Liz stood on the road side at Mahone Bay, watching a man named Marty focus his camera on three graceful churches which cast their reflections across the shimmering water.

"Got it!" Marty said, then hurried back to his car. "Let's move out, kids. Time is short."

He jumped into the passenger seat, and his wife burned rubber as soon as the rear door slammed behind Tom and Liz. Professor Zinck smiled at the couple in the front seat.

"Chris and Marty," he said, "let me thank you again for offering a drive to total strangers. When my wife was taken ill, I was afraid our trip would have to be cancelled."

25

"I'm glad Tom and Liz explained you were stuck for a ride," Chris said, her attractive eyes smiling at the Professor in the mirror. "We absolutely *must* shoot Peggy's Cove first, then we'll visit Oak Island with you to check out all this hoopla about pirates."

"After that we'll hit Chester and Hubbards Beach," Marty said, consulting a list of tourist attractions. Picking up his calculator, he punched in distances and checked these against his watch. The young New Jersey couple had arrived as guests at "The Fisherman's Home" the previous evening, and were determined to photograph every possible attraction before returning to the States.

"I love this place!" Marty exclaimed. "Do you know that people never lock their doors here? It's amazing!"

"And the scenery is magnificent," Chris said. "Look at the view coming up now."

The highway ran beside the sea. The deep blue of the water was separated from the pale blue of the sky by a distant headland, shadowed by the morning sun climbing behind it. Close to shore was the silhouette of a girl in a rowboat, pulling in a net as her collie watched alertly from the bow.

"Let's get this scene," Marty said.

The car screeched to a stop. As Marty fiddled with his camera, Tom watched two gulls squabbling noisily over a tasty morsel. One of them lifted away into the sky, dipped and soared, then circled down to a log bleached white by the sun. Its smooth texture reminded Tom of the smooth leather case containing Black Dog's treasures.

"I hope Mrs. Zinck will be better soon, Professor."

He responded with a brief smile. "Thank you."

"You don't seem yourself."

"You're right." The Professor waited for the car to get under way, then looked at Tom and Liz. "Please forgive my mood. I had a forerunner last night, and it left me a bit shaken."

"What's a forerunner?"

"I'd rather not discuss it, Liz."

She stared intently at the Professor. "It's a superstition, isn't it? That's why you won't tell me. You think I'll faint or something."

He shook his head. "Of course not. The subject upsets me, that's all."

Liz sat back, and gazed moodily at the passing scene. At times Marty's camera clicked, and once Tom yawned, but all was peaceful until Chris suddenly swung the wheel. The car bounced and fish-tailed along the highway shoulder, then swerved back onto the asphalt.

"What happened?" Professor Zinck shouted in panic.

"Some jerk came speeding around the corner on our side. Boy, did that scare me!"

"Good driving, honey," Marty said quietly. "You saved our bacon."

Sweat glistened on the Professor's forehead. He wiped at it with a shaking hand, then leaned forward to watch for more trouble. "I should never have come today," he muttered to himself. "First Arnold Smith, and now me."

"Professor Zinck, *please* tell us! What is a fore-runner?"

"It's a warning of approaching death."

"*What*?"

"Now, aren't you sorry you asked?" The Professor shook his head. "Some things are better left alone."

"What kind of a warning? Do you hear voices?"

"No."

"Well, what then?"

Professor Zinck sighed. "Very well, Liz, I give up. I'll tell you about forerunners, and then let's drop the subject."

"Agreed."

"A person might hear three slow taps on the wall, and shortly after someone in the family dies. Or a forerunner could take the form of seeing your own spirit. I heard of a woman who was passing a cemetery and saw a ghostly vision of herself, walking among the tombstones. She went home, gave away her possessions, and died shortly after."

"I can't stand it." Liz hugged her body, but kept her eyes fixed on the Professor. "Tell us more."

"Arnold Smith was a teacher who drove this way to school. One night, without warning, people appeared on the road ahead and he just missed hitting them. Arnold got out of his car, but they'd disappeared into thin air."

"How was that a forerunner?"

"A week later, Arnold himself was killed when his car plunged off the road."

28

"I don't get it."

"Arnold's car crashed at the exact spot where he'd seen the ghostly people. They were his forerunner, warning him that he was about to die."

"I feel faint." For a moment Liz stared at the Professor with wide eyes, then she remembered something. "Hey! What about *your* forerunner, Professor?"

"I won't discuss it, Liz, and that's final."

"You win." She smiled. "Thanks for telling me about forerunners, anyway. I guess I'll be listening tonight for three slow taps on the wall, but I still had to know."

"Hey folks," Marty said, looking puzzled, "why haven't we seen a Mountie yet?"

"There's one straight ahead."

"*What?*" he shouted, grabbing his camera. "Where? I don't see one!"

"In that police car."

"But he's wearing a brown uniform. And where's his horse?"

Tom laughed. "Mounties patrol in cars these days, and they only wear red serge for special occasions."

Marty lowered his camera. "What a disappointment! How can I face everyone back home, without a picture of a genuine Mountie?"

"Check the Legislative Building in Halifax. There may be one there in dress uniform."

"Let's hope so." Marty looked at a highway sign, announcing the approach to Peggy's Cove.

"What if this place lets us down, too? It may not even have a lighthouse. I'll be stuck with a bunch of empty film!"

Chris gave him an affectionate smile. "I'm sure it's going to be beautiful, sweetheart."

This was an accurate prediction. The car entered a spectacular landscape of treeless land, empty of anything but the wandering highway and hundreds of huge boulders scattered everywhere. Some lay alone, others balanced against each other, resting exactly where they'd been left thousands of years ago by the melting of an Ice Age glacier.

"In parts of Nova Scotia the ice was two kilometres high," Professor Zinck said. "Here the glacier scraped away all the soil, exposing granite that is 415 million years old."

"Give or take a year."

He smiled. "There's Peggy's Cove, straight ahead. Don't the houses look fragile out on the granite?"

"You'd think the first good wind would blow them into the sea!"

Houses of bright blues and yellows and reds were perched above the waves. The village was dominated by a church spire and the famous lighthouse. Chris followed a lane which wound among the houses, needing all her driving skills to avoid the hundreds of tourists who clogged the village.

"That poor kid," Liz said, looking at a girl who'd stepped onto the porch of her house and been instantly photographed. "Imagine living in the middle of a tourist trap."

"This is fantastic." Marty grabbed his camera as the car stopped in a parking lot beside a tour bus from Ontario. "We're scheduled for thirty minutes here, so let's hustle."

The young couple hurried off. Professor Zinck wanted to stay in the car, so Tom and Liz headed alone across the granite toward the booming surf.

"Maybe the Professor's forerunner warned him not to walk out here," Tom said, pointing at a sign which cautioned *swells and breaking waves may unexpectedly rise over the rocks and sweep you out to sea*.

Liz snorted. "You get full marks for imagination."

"Well, something is bothering Professor Zinck."

"Sure, he's upset about the forerunner. Plus Mrs. Zinck being sick."

"Now, *that* is definitely weird. Just last night Mrs. Zinck told us she's frightened, and today she's on death's door."

Liz laughed. "She's probably got flu, or a sore tummy from too much Solomon Gundy."

Tom jumped between two slabs of granite, then studied the many fissures which seamed the rock like the face of a very old person. "Just like the lines on Henneyberry's face. I'll bet he put something in Mrs. Zinck's food, and that's why she's out of commission."

"But why? You're always producing a theory before you have any proof. You should study the situation, watch the people, and only speak up when you've got an iron-clad case."

"You work your way, Liz, and I'll work mine."

As they approached the lighthouse, the wind carried the click of cameras and the shouts of tourists setting up pictures: *Move to your left—NO!—I said your LEFT! Can't you get that kid to smile? Hey, lady, you're blocking my shot!* People from tour buses, wearing plastic name tags, filed into the lighthouse to investigate its tiny post office. Tom checked it out, then sat with Liz in the warm sunshine until their time was up. Right on the minute, their car rolled out of Peggy's Cove past a final vision of a wharf which was piled high with lobster traps and groaning under the weight of a multitude of cameras and their owners.

"Whoever designed this village must have received a fat fee from Kodak."

Tom laughed briefly at the joke, then noticed a highway sign that had been riddled with bullets. Could this be a forerunner, warning him of his own death? Was he about to die on Oak Island, so far from home?

Hoping Liz wouldn't notice, he got out his lucky coin and rubbed it vigorously.

"I guess nobody's actually been killed there?"

Professor Zinck looked at Tom. "Killed where?"

"At Oak Island."

"Actually, five men have died while searching for the treasure that is supposed to be at the bottom of the Money Pit. In 1860 a man was scalded to death when a pumping machine blew up, and in 1963 four more were overcome by fumes while working in an excavation. The locals say only one more must die, and then the island will give up its secret. But of course that's just superstition."

"Sure," Tom said, trying to smile.

"Say Prof," Marty asked, "is it true that Captain Kidd buried his horde on Oak Island?"

"No one knows. Just before his execution, Kidd offered to reveal the secret location of his treasure in return for a pardon. He said there'd be enough gold to make a chain that would stretch around the city of London, but the authorities refused the deal and hung him."

"What exactly is this Money Pit?"

"It was discovered by a teenager way back in 1795. He was hunting on the island and spotted an ancient ship's tackle-block dangling from the branch of an oak. The ground below had caved in slightly, so the boy figured something might be buried there and came back with a couple of friends and some shovels. They made a discovery that led to what has become the most expensive treasure hunt in history."

"They found gold?"

"No, they discovered a circular shaft with walls of solid clay, and a floor of oaken planks. They ripped these out, and what do you suppose they found?"

"More dirt?"

"Exactly. Down they went, and soon they came to a second set of planks. When these were removed they kept on digging, and found yet another platform!"

"Those poor guys. How discouraging."

"Apparently they were very excited, because it

33

appeared that something of immense value must be down there. Otherwise why build all those elaborate platforms? Eventually, with the help of others, they had removed nine platforms and were down very deep when they struck something hard which stretched the width of the shaft. They were convinced the treasure lay directly beneath, but it was getting dark so they climbed back up to the surface and spent a happy evening discussing how they'd spend the money."

"What did they find the next day?" Liz asked.

"A shaft full of water." The Professor shook his head in sympathy with the long-ago treasure searchers. "They started to bale water, then used a pump, but the pit remained flooded. Eventually it was discovered that the engineering genius who constructed the Money Pit had included a second shaft that angled out to the sea bed. This was designed to flood the Money Pit if strangers got into it, and the plan worked! The first searchers gave up, but many others have tried ever since. There have been twenty-one separate shafts dug, even though nothing has been brought up so far except three links of a gold watch chain."

Liz smiled. "What a great story. In a way I hope no one discovers the truth, because it's more fun to wonder what's down there."

Tom looked down the highway, where a sign with a huge pirate indicated the turn-off to Oak Island. "The secret is safe until one more person dies," he said with a doom-laden voice.

"You're becoming superstitious, Tom!"

"Yeah? Well, this place sounds creepy."

The car bumped along a narrow causeway toward Oak Island, which appeared peaceful enough. Another giant pirate, holding a treasure chest on his shoulder, stood guard with a cutlass outside a building marked *tickets*. Chris parked beside a black van with two skulls on the rear door, and they were crossing the lot when a familiar face emerged from the woods.

"It's Roger Eliot-Stanton," Liz said. "You wouldn't think he'd be interested in Oak Island."

"I bet he won't even say hello."

Sure enough, their fellow guest from "The Fisherman's Home" hurried across the parking lot and passed them without a word.

"Why *is* he here?" Tom said. "Maybe we should follow him."

Liz laughed. "As much as I dislike the guy, I can't believe he's a criminal. He's just a tourist, like the rest of us."

Tom watched the long-legged man open a car door, then look their way. "Ah ha! He did see us. Why did he pretend not to?"

"He's just being rude," Liz said. "Doesn't he look dumb with that gold ear-ring?"

Chris smiled. "I think it makes him look very handsome. It's so unusual."

"Unusual is right! Another word might be gross!"

They walked along a narrow dirt road through the woods past sweet-smelling evergreens, thickly carpeted ferns and flowering bushes. A strange fear grew in Tom that danger lay ahead, but he overcame it by picturing the three boys as they walked across this very island centuries ago on their way to making such a great discovery.

"Do you believe in the Money Pit, Professor Zinck?"

"Something may be down there, Tom. One writer suggested it could hold the combined wealth of several famous pirates, including Blackbeard and Morgan, but of course that's just a guess."

"It's strange they would leave it behind on a deserted island without any guards."

"People say that after pirates buried a treasure, they often chopped off someone's head and threw him down the hole so his ghost would be on guard. The belief is that buried treasure can only be dug up at night, and if anyone speaks during the expedition the guardian ghost will be given the power to rise up and slay the treasure seekers."

"What a way to die."

The road emerged from the woods at a bay with a rocky beach. A pink shell near the water attracted Liz's attention, and Chris commented on the cool breeze off the sea, but Tom's eyes were drawn to a nearby hill where a tall drilling rig stood dramatically against the sky.

"There it is! The treasure site, and they're still searching!"

"I don't think anyone's there right now," Professor Zinck said. "I read in the paper that they're waiting for new equipment to arrive."

The group hurried along the beach and started climbing toward the rig, but the Professor held up a hand before they'd reached it.

"We're at the original Money Pit."

Confused, Tom looked around the hillside and then spotted a few tumbled-down timbers surrounding a hole full of dirt. "This is *it*?"

The Professor nodded. "Are you disappointed?"

"A bit."

Tom stared down into the hole, then continued up the hill to the rig. It stood directly above a large steel pipe which reached deep down into the earth. Tom dropped a pebble and heard it hit water somewhere far below. Straightening up, he studied the rusty machinery which was scattered around. The door of a tarpaper shack slammed back and forth in the wind that rushed across the hilltop, and a rusting car without wheels stood under a tree, but the scene was empty of life.

"It's like a ghost camp," Liz said.

"I like it here. It's neat to think of all the people who've gone after the treasure. Just think, Liz, Captain Kidd's gold may be right under our feet!"

Professor Zinck came up the hill, puffing from the strain of the climb, but Chris and Marty weren't with him. "They've gone to Chester," the Professor explained. "They'll collect us in an hour."

"What else can we see?"

He pointed toward a cove. "Down there is the 'G rock' which was discovered in 1970. Maybe you can figure out what it means."

"Are you coming with us?"

"No thanks. Climbing up and down hills isn't my cup of tea."

A letter G had been chiselled into the rock, but

there was no way of knowing what it could mean. "G stands for gold," Tom suggested. "Maybe the treasure is buried here!"

"G also means ghouls, ghosts and goblins. Let's turn the rock over, and see what comes screeching out."

"Forget it." Tom skipped some flat stones across the ocean, then they started up the hill toward the rig. "We may be walking in the footsteps of pirates, Liz. Can't you just picture a ship with a Jolly Roger anchored in the cove, and men with eye-patches and cutlasses climbing this very hill with treasure chests for the Money Pit. What drama!"

"I've had enough drama for one day, what with the Professor's forerunner and nearly getting killed on the highway. This place is getting on my nerves. I keep expecting a headless pirate to leap out at us."

There was no sign of Professor Zinck at the top of the hill. The whistle of the wind in the drilling rig, and the banging of the tarpaper door, made Tom feel lonely as he looked around for their friend.

"There's something wrong, Liz. I can feel it."

"Where's Professor Zinck?"

"I don't know, but he wouldn't leave without telling us." Tom glanced at the scattered equipment, then tried to see into the darkness within the shack. He felt certain that someone was watching them, and was about to tell Liz when there was a flurry of sound from the woods.

Whirling around, he saw a black raven rise

above the trees and head out to sea. The sudden fright made the blood pound through his veins, and he watched anxiously as Liz walked past the machinery to look down the hillside. Somehow he knew that she would turn and call his name.

Liz turned, her face shocked. "Tom! Come here!"

With a feeling that he was living through a horrible dream, Tom stumbled over bits of rusty metal and old machinery, then ran to Liz's side and looked toward the Money Pit. Professor Zinck lay beside it, face down in the dirt.

# 4

Tom and Liz rushed to the Professor, and found blood seeping from a wound in his temple. Gently they rolled him over, and Liz checked for a pulse beat.

"Look at this!" Tom said, kneeling down. "He managed to write something in the dirt before passing out."

Clearly visible in the dirt were the letters EVEL. Liz looked at them, then stood up. "We've got to get help!"

They ran quickly through the woods to the ticket office, and breathlessly asked the attendant for assistance. Saying that she had first-aid training, the attendant drove them back across the island in her jeep, and the trio raced to the Money Pit.

Professor Zinck was gone.

"I don't understand," Tom stammered, staring at the Money Pit. "He was lying right beside it."

"Is this a practical joke?" the attendant said, frowning.

"No, ma'am! You can see the dirt's all mussed up, where Professor Zinck was lying. And look where he wrote EVEL."

The attendant returned to the jeep, shaking her head. Feeling embarrassed and worried, Tom and Liz remained at the Money Pit to search for the Professor, but found no sign of him, either in the surrounding trees or the tarpaper shack.

"Maybe he was dazed, and wandered away through the woods."

"We could never search an island this big. Let's wait at the parking lot until Chris and Marty get back, and see what they think."

At the lot Tom and Liz paced anxiously, wondering what might have happened. Who had attacked Professor Zinck, and why had he then disappeared?

"That was a clue he wrote in the dirt," Tom said. "He was telling us he'd been attacked by Evil, or something like that. He just spelled it wrong."

"A professor can't spell the word evil?"

"You've got a point. But I'm sure EVEL is a clue."

At long last, Chris and Marty rolled into the

41

parking lot. The smiles quickly left their faces when they heard the news, but Chris had a hopeful suggestion.

"Maybe he walked through the woods while you were fetching the attendant, and then talked some driver into giving him a ride home. If he was dazed, he might have forgotten about meeting us."

"You think he's gone back to Lunenburg?"

"It's possible. Why don't we drive there and find out?"

Although reluctant to leave Oak Island without the Professor, Tom and Liz agreed to check his home before contacting the police about a search party. When they reached Lunenburg they were taken to the Manor by Chris and Marty, who waited in the car.

"Please be home, Professor!" Tom said, as the doorbell echoed somewhere deep within Lunenburg Manor.

The door creaked open. "Yes?" Henneyberry said mournfully.

"Mr. Henneyberry, is the Professor here?"

"Yes."

"Really?" Liz smiled happily. "I don't believe it! We've been worried sick."

Henneyberry started to close the door, but Tom stopped him. "Please, sir, can we talk to Professor Zinck? We'd like to know what happened."

Henneyberry shook his head. "The Professor is not feeling well."

"How about if we come back later, after we see the police?"

"Why are you going to the police?"

"Professor Zinck was attacked at Oak Island. We've got to report it. They'll want to question him, and start an investigation."

"I see," Henneyberry said, nodding slowly. "Well, come back here after you've been to the police."

Tom and Liz hurried down the porch steps, and had almost reached the car when Henneyberry called their names. As he beckoned them back to the Manor, they exchanged puzzled glances.

"What is it, Mr. Henneyberry?"

"I've decided that you should talk to Professor Zinck before seeing the police. He may want the officers to come here, and question you all together."

"That's a good idea."

"But do remember that the Professor's had a terrible shock. He's not himself."

Henneyberry led them into the shadowy hallway, then up the tower stairs. Light filtered in through stained-glass windows cheerfully decorated with flowers and birds, but the atmosphere was still gloomy as they followed Henneyberry's slow-motion steps to the top floor and along a dark hallway. At the end of the hall were some service stairs, and a closed bedroom door.

"Wait here," Henneyberry whispered. He went into the bedroom, and shut the door.

"I wonder how Mrs. Zinck is feeling?"

"I'm not surprised she's afraid of this spooky old place. When the Professor tells her about the attack, she's going to be even more worried."

Tom looked at an old painting on the wall, then began pacing the hallway. At last, Henneyberry opened the door. "Don't be too long."

Musty hot air filled the room, and a fireplace threw dancing light on the walls. The Professor lay in a four-poster bed topped by an elaborate canopy. Beyond the bed was a circular alcove with windows looking down to the harbour and the boats riding at anchor.

Professor Zinck lifted his head from the pillow, and they saw a large bandage over his temple. Raising a weak hand, he motioned for Tom and Liz to come forward.

"Many thanks for your concern," he said, his voice no more than a whisper.

"Who attacked you, Professor?"

"My mind's a blank. I remember talking to you near the drilling rig, and then all I have is a brief memory of riding in a car. Apparently I walked to the highway and flagged down a motorist, who brought me home. I can't remember anything else."

Henneyberry fussed with the pillow in an effort to make the Professor comfortable, then poured him a glass of water. "The doctor says you'll be fine after a few days' rest."

"Professor Zinck, have you called the police yet?"

"I'm not going to."

"But why not?"

"It will upset my wife, who's already ill. First the police will come here, then there'll be a news story and the neighbours will be calling. Once started, it never ends. Do you understand?"

44

Liz nodded. "I see your point. But what about the attack? Shouldn't it be investigated?"

"I must think of my wife."

"Then *we'll* investigate it, Professor!"

He looked concerned. "I'd rather you didn't. There's been enough trouble."

"Don't worry," Tom said. "We can look after ourselves, and you've already given us a great lead to work on."

"I have?" The Professor attempted a smile. "Impossible."

"Do you remember writing EVEL in the dirt?"

He looked startled. "What?"

"We're sure it's a clue to your attacker! Don't you remember?"

Looking pale, Professor Zinck frowned in concentration. "No, I'm sorry, but nothing comes back."

"You're straining yourself, sir," Henneyberry warned. "You should rest now."

"Perhaps you're right."

Liz smiled at him. "It's great you're safe, Professor. We'll try to find out who attacked you."

As they followed Henneyberry down the stairs, Tom pictured Mrs. Zinck lying ill somewhere in the house. Why was she suddenly so sick? With a shudder, he thought of her fears about the Manor. Were they about to come true?

\* \* \*

The next morning, Tom tried to convince Chris and Marty to return to Oak Island in search of clues, but the young couple had only a few days' holiday and they were anxious to see the Annapolis Valley. When Liz accepted Shirley's invitation to visit Lunenburg's Fisheries Museum, Tom had to stifle a groan. A *museum*, when there was a mystery to solve!

Happily, visiting the museum unexpectedly solved the problem of how to return to Oak Island. While boarding the schooner *Theresa E. Connor*, one of the historical vessels docked at the museum, Shirley called hello to a young man examining the dories on the schooner's deck. Introduced as "Cap'n John," he turned out to be a friend of Professor and Mrs. Zinck.

"How terrible!" he said, after hearing a description of the attack on Oak Island. "Is there anything I can do to help?"

"Would you drive us there, to search for leads?"

"How about going by sea?"

"Fantastic! Let's get moving!" Glancing at Shirley's disappointed face, Tom realized he was being rude. "I mean, after we've seen this schooner."

Cap'n John agreed to the plan, then walked forward with them to the schooner's bow. His pride in being from Lunenburg was soon obvious, as was his love of the sea and the great schooners which had once sailed from here to the Grand Banks of Newfoundland.

"Boys as young as ten went to sea as 'headers,' meaning their job was to cut the heads off the fish. They would get up with the rest of the men at 2 a.m. for breakfast, then row out in the dories despite blizzards and howling winds. The tragedy was that they often never made it back. The bones of many men are out there still."

"Why did they drown?"

"Because of the terrible weather. Imagine two men in a dory, lost in a heavy fog, trying to fight their way toward the sound of the cannon which signalled from the schooner, while the seas broke over them from every direction. It was a hard life."

Shirley looked up at the signal flags, snapping in the wind. "The greatest schooner of all was the *Bluenose*, which was built in Lunenburg and was world champion in the races they held for these ships."

"Say kids," Cap'n John said. "If you've got a dollar, I can sell you a terrific souvenir of the *Bluenose*."

"Great!" Tom produced a crumpled dollar, then frowned as Cap'n John handed him a dime. "What's this?"

"Your souvenir. On the back of that dime you'll see the *Bluenose* in full sail."

Tom stared in dismay at the coin, then the others burst into laughter and a grinning Cap'n John returned his money.

"Never trust a stranger with your cash," he said, chuckling. "By the way, Tom, there's a great picture of Lunenburg and its schooners on the hundred-dollar bill. I can get you one for only $200."

The jokes continued until the tour was over, and they'd said goodbye to Shirley on the dock.

Cap'n John led the way past the harbour's bright-red buildings to a dock where they climbed down into a skiff. With waves slapping against it, the skiff headed toward the many boats riding at anchor in the harbour.

"Which is yours, Cap'n John?"

Resting over the oars, he pointed to one with a sign reading *Island Tours*. "There it is," he said, smiling proudly. "I've converted it to take tourists out to visit some of the islands in Mahone Bay. Business isn't very good right now, but it'll improve!"

"What if it doesn't?" Liz asked anxiously. "Will you be ruined?"

He laughed. "Let's hope not. I can always go to the Grand Banks on a trawler, but then I'd hardly ever see my family. Anyway, in the past little while I've managed to rent my boat to locals a couple of times, so things look good!"

On board the tour boat, Liz went into the cabin to watch Cap'n John start up the engine, while Tom sat in the stern, enjoying the lapping of waves against the hull and the light wind on his face. Nova Scotia sure was great, he thought, even if weird things did seem to happen here. The riddle of Oak Island, the superstitions and fore-runners, the icy fingers that had brushed his neck and the attack on Professor Zinck—they were all puzzles that seemed to have no answers. What did it all mean? Who or what was causing these strange things to happen?

The powerful engine came alive, and Liz

emerged to sit in the sunshine as the boat headed out of Lunenburg harbour.

"Isn't Cap'n John gorgeous?" she whispered. "His hair must get so blond from all the time he spends in the sun. Thank goodness I got my new contact lenses before our trip."

Tom sighed, and rolled his eyes to heaven. "Not another crush! At least this one's better than that weird-o, Black Dog. That creep could star in a commercial for a funeral parlour. *Come to us when you look like me.*"

Liz shook her head in disgust, and went back inside. After a while Tom followed her into the cabin. Liz sat on one of the benches which faced the thudding engine, listening to Cap'n John describe his hobby of diving to shipwrecks.

"Not long ago I brought up a very special treasure. Buttons, from an 1853 wreck. Maybe you wouldn't think buttons are beautiful, but these were polished stones of most unusual shapes. There's a precious one of green jade that I'm saving for my little girl."

"I love the sea," said Liz. "It makes me feel so peaceful. When I'm older I think I'll take up scuba-diving."

"It's a great experience." Cap'n John looked out at a sailboat, leaning far to starboard under the wind, then checked his chart. "We're not far from Oak Island. Look, over there."

Tom and Liz looked toward the shore, where the drilling rig on Oak Island grew slowly out of the waves. At Smugglers Cove they glided in over a transparent sea that revealed dark green eel-grass, waving gently below the surface. The beach was littered with jelly fish, shimmering brown blobs which Cap'n John said were composed mainly of water.

As they walked along the path toward the drilling rig, Cap'n John pointed out the damsel flies which darted around their dusty feet, then stopped at a plant with purple flowers and red berries. "Eating two of those berries will stop your heart."

"Impossible." Tom picked two berries, lifted them to his mouth, and started chewing. "You see? Nothing's happening."

Cap'n John gasped in shock. "Spit them out! They'll kill you!"

Tom opened his hand to reveal the red berries. "I didn't forget your trick about the dime," he said, grinning.

Cap'n John laughed, and pounded Tom's back with a friendly hand. "You got me, fair and square! Now let's see what kind of a detective you are."

Tom nodded, determined to find some clue to help their investigation. After checking the Money Pit, he climbed the hill and stared at the piles of rusty machinery. What a mess! It would take *hours* to check through it, and he didn't even know what to look for.

As he tried to think of an easier approach, Tom watched his sister carefully examining the ground around the tarpaper shack. He felt a little annoyed. If he didn't hustle, soon Liz would find a clue, and he'd look bad. Quickly, Tom began digging among the tangles of old buckets and ladders and tools.

Finding nothing but rust, he straightened up and tried to think. Where could an attacker have hidden yesterday? The woods, the shack or inside the old wrecked car were the only possibilities.

The woods were too large to search and Liz was already inside the shack, but that still left the car. Suddenly hopeful, Tom headed toward it just as Liz came out of the shack.

"Nothing in here," she said, sounding discouraged.

"Nobody's checked the woods yet."

As Liz looked at the trees, Tom tried to find a route through the piles of machinery to the car. But he kept getting blocked, and he knew Liz would think of checking the car at any moment.

"Say, Liz, isn't that something in the shack?"

"Where?"

"On the floor, way in the back. Looks a bit like a gun, or maybe a knife?"

Liz went inside the shack, and for a wild moment Tom was tempted to slam the door and lock her in. Then at last he got free of the machinery, and dashed to the car.

"Tom, what are you doing? What's in the car?"

"Nothing! Get away from here!"

"Do you think someone was hiding in the car yesterday? What a brainwave!"

"Take off, Liz! This is my car."

Liz opened the front door, and watched Tom search around the pedals and under the seat.

"Found anything?"

"Would I still be looking?"

"Let's try the back seat."

"Listen, Liz, this car was my idea. Get out of here!"

Liz tried to open the rear door, but the rusty metal screeched and refused to move. As she yanked on the door, Tom scrambled into the back seat and landed in thick dust. For a moment he was blinded, then he heard a rusty squeal as Liz got the door open. Wiping his eyes, he saw the glint of shiny metal on the floor. His hand flashed down, and snatched up a set of keys just as Liz reached for them.

"You shouldn't touch them, Tom! They may have fingerprints."

"Tough."

"Put them back on the floor!"

"And have you grab them? Not a chance." Tightly holding the keys, Tom crawled out of the car. "Hey, this really *is* a clue. Liz! Look at the initials on the key-ring."

"CZ." Liz nodded her head. "Those are Professor Zinck's initials. He must have been inside the car after the attack."

"But why?"

"I don't know, Tom. But this whole thing gets stranger by the minute."

"And scarier." Tom stared at the keys in his hand. "I keep thinking about Mrs. Zinck, and the Professor's forerunner. I have this awful feeling that something terrible is about to happen and we won't be able to stop it."

\* \* \*

52

Cap'n John's boat arrived in Lunenburg shortly before nightfall, giving Tom and Liz time to return the Professor's keys before going back to Stonehurst.

At the Manor, they slowly followed Henneyberry up the tower stairs and along the gloomy hallway toward Professor Zinck's bedroom. Lying outside the door was his Irish setter, Boss, looking sad.

"What's wrong, boy?" Tom said, kneeling down. "Why aren't you inside, close to your master?" He pulled gently on the dog's collar, trying to coax it toward the door, but Boss held back, whining.

Suddenly Tom heard the familiar voice of Roger Eliot-Stanton, coming from behind the closed door. "I can make it worth your while. Name your price!"

There was a moment's pause, then Professor Zinck spoke. "I don't have a price. I will never agree."

The door banged open, and Roger Eliot-Stanton appeared. Briefly he stared toward the Professor, firelight on his deeply hollowed face. Then, without saying a word to Tom and Liz, his long legs carried him away.

"What a nerd," Liz whispered. "I've never met such a rude man. What's he doing here, anyway?"

The Professor managed a smile when they entered the bedroom, but he was obviously still not himself. His eyes were strained, and his mind seemed to wander to other thoughts as Tom and Liz described their search at Oak Island.

"And Tom found your keys!" Liz said excitedly. "It's a great clue, because it tells us your location after the attack."

Professor Zinck looked vaguely at the keys, then handed them to Henneyberry. "I'm in no shape to drive, so you'll have to do the errands."

"Very well, sir."

The Professor gazed into the fireplace for some time. Finally he seemed to remember that Tom and Liz were present, and turned to them with troubled eyes. "Have you enjoyed the company of an old professor?"

"You bet! We just hope you get well soon."

"Of course, of course." There was a long silence, followed by a sigh. "Life or death. What will the decision be?"

Tom frowned, wondering if the Professor was feverish. Henneyberry fluffed up his pillow, and tried to smile. "It will all work out, sir. Try to relax."

"Relax?" The Professor laughed, but it was a horrible sound that made Tom's skin crawl. "Relax, you say? When life hangs by a thread?"

The creases around Henneyberry's eyes deepened. "There's nothing to worry about, sir. Leave everything to me."

Professor Zinck slumped down on the pillow, and his eyes focussed on the yellow flame of a candle beside his bed. "How easily I could snuff that out."

Looking very worried, Liz reached out to touch the Professor's hand. "How is your wife feeling?"

Professor Zinck looked blank. "My wife?"

Henneyberry put a warning hand on Liz's shoulder. "Try to rest, sir," he said, then led Tom and Liz away from the bed. They had a final glimpse of the Professor's troubled face before the door closed, and Henneyberry shook his head.

"I've been terribly concerned, but the doctor says the worst will soon be over."

"How *is* Mrs. Zinck?"

"Not well, I'm afraid. At times she's as delirious as the Professor, and says some very strange things."

As Henneyberry showed Tom and Liz to the front door, the bell rang and he admitted a woman dressed in expensive clothes. Obviously used to his slow pace, she refused to be led upstairs, and hurried on alone. Without waiting for Tom and Liz to leave, an anxious-looking Henneyberry went after her.

"What's going on in this place?" Tom said. "The Professor's acting so weird."

"I wonder who that woman is? And what was Roger Eliot-Stanton doing here?"

"I don't trust that beanpole, Liz. Yesterday we saw him at Oak Island just before the attack, and today he's at the Manor. What's the connection?"

"Maybe he . . ." Liz paused, and her eyes widened. "Did you hear that?"

"Hear what?"

Liz stared along the shadowed hallway. "I'm sure I heard footsteps," she whispered. "It was like someone on tip-toe."

"Let's get out of here, Liz! I don't like this place."

55

"Look!"

At the end of the hallway, the door of the sitting room was slowly opening. As Tom and Liz watched, horrified, a white hand appeared, and beckoned.

# 5

Tom's heart pounded. "It's the ghost!"

"No," Liz said, squinting. "It's Mrs. Zinck. What does she want?"

The hand motioned frantically, then a warning finger went to Mrs. Zinck's lips as Tom and Liz approached. As they stepped into the room she closed the door, and turned to them with a haggard face.

"I'm so afraid!"

"What's wrong, Mrs. Zinck?"

"It's this house. Something terrible is happening here."

Tom remembered Henneyberry saying that Mrs. Zinck had been delirious, and wondered whether she was hallucinating now. Then he recalled how frightened she had been of the Manor even before she became ill.

"And it's the Professor," Mrs. Zinck said, drawing her bathrobe tight at the neck with shaking fingers. "He frightens me."

"But he's your husband!"

"Even so, I'm afraid of him. This morning when I went to his room for a visit he hardly seemed to know me, and just lay there muttering about life and death."

"We heard that, too."

"Then he demanded that I leave the room. He said I was making him feel guilty, of all things."

Tom looked at the grandfather clock, ticking in a corner of the lonely room. He wished he knew how to comfort Mrs. Zinck. "I'm sure he'll be better soon," he said at last.

"Oh, I hope so!" Mrs. Zinck smiled, but tears were in her eyes. "This afternoon, I went to see him again. As I reached the bedroom, I heard him making arrangements with Henneyberry for the lawyer to visit. That's the woman who just arrived."

"Why a lawyer?"

"My husband is removing Black Dog from his will. It's absolutely insane, because he loves Black Dog like a son. I'm so afraid that some evil power has possessed him, but what can I do?"

"We'll try to help you, Mrs. Zinck."

Outside the Manor, Tom and Liz paused in the darkness to look up at the Professor's bedroom. The flickering firelight cast the long shadow of Henneyberry on the wall, and for a terrible moment Tom wondered whether the man was a demon who'd somehow taken control of Professor Zinck.

"That's stupid!" he said aloud. "But there must be some reason for what's happening."

"You're right," Liz agreed. "So let's decide who'd want to harm the Zincks."

"Black Dog!"

"Are you nuts? We just heard that the Professor loves him like a son."

"But does Black Dog love the Professor?"

"Of course he does."

"You're just saying that because of your crush on Black Dog. Remember, he gets the Zincks' money if they die."

"And you're just saying that because you don't like him."

Tom fell silent, refusing to give in, then gave a stone an angry kick as they started walking. "This is my case, Liz, so I don't care if you help, or stay home reading a book."

"*Your case*?"

"That's right. I found the Professor's keys at Oak Island, and that puts me in charge."

"I saw those keys before you, but I couldn't get the car door open."

"Sure, sure. Anyway, I'm going to break this case wide open, with your help or without it."

They walked on in silence, until finally Liz glanced at Tom. "O.K., let's hear your argument against Black Dog."

"Well, if the Professor knows that Black Dog attacked him at the Money Pit, it would explain why he's being removed from the will. And the Professor is terrified of another attack by Black Dog, which accounts for him raving about life and death."

"O.K., I admit that *maybe* you've got something. Should we go to the police?"

Tom thought for a minute. "No, we'd better not. The Professor doesn't want the police involved, and we don't want him feeling any worse."

"Then what should we do?"

"I read in a detective manual that a good way to learn something about your suspect is to spring a surprise. Let's drop in on Black Dog tomorrow afternoon for an unexpected visit."

"Isn't that taking a chance?"

Tom smiled. "Black Dog works in the school's boiler room, doesn't he? What could be safer than a school?"

\* \* \*

The confidence of Tom's statement was badly shaken the next day, however, when he learned that the school was located at the top of Gallows Hill. Climbing the hill, Tom and Liz found themselves approaching the school through a cemetery full of moss-covered tombstones and twisted old trees.

"Is *that* it?" Liz asked, staring at an ancient building with narrow windows and pointed bell-towers. "It looks like something out of a horror movie."

"Ha ha," Tom said nervously. "I think it's very nice. Imagine going to school here!"

"The mind boggles." Liz looked at the fog, which had rolled in from the sea an hour before and was blowing through the trees like smoke.

"What a day to be investigating a creaky old school that even has its own graveyard."

"Are you ready to go inside?"

"No!" Liz watched the fog swirling past the school's towers. "You know what happens when Lunenburg kids fail a test? They get locked away in those towers, with spiders and rats to gnaw on their bones."

Tom managed a smile; his determination to investigate Black Dog was quickly fading away. "These are interesting tombstones," he said, letting his feet walk away from the school. "Why don't we poke around the cemetery a bit, then try the school tomorrow?"

"Carl said the weather's going to turn bad. Do you want to come back here in a storm?"

Pretending not to hear, Tom studied a tombstone that showed a hand pointing to heaven and the words *Gone Home*. Nearby were two stones with the names of fishermen lost from schooners. Looking around, he became aware of how many people from Lunenburg had drowned at sea.

There also seemed to be a lot of mossy stones marking the graves of children. One family had lost several at birth, including twin boys.

"That's sad," Liz said, leaning close to read the tombstone, which was covered in places with patches of mustard-yellow moss. "If they'd become grownup twins, I wonder if they'd have looked the same. You know, wearing matching clothes and all that."

Tom shrugged. "I've never seen identical adult twins."

"Look at this one." Liz kneeled in front of a very old stone which was dark with age. Engraved on it were lilies and the name of Mary Eliza Rudolf, who died in 1849 at the age of ten. "She was a Liz, just like me. I wonder what she was like?"

Leaving Liz to think about Mary Eliza, Tom walked around studying tombstones and trying to figure out the story of each person from names and dates. The name Zinck appeared often, and Tom realized how many generations of the family must have lived in Lunenburg Manor.

Raising his eyes from a black marble *Zinck* tombstone, Tom stared at the school, knowing that the lives of Professor and Mrs. Zinck could depend on their investigation of Black Dog. He waved at Liz, still in front of Mary Eliza's tombstone. "I'm going into the school!"

"Wait for me." Standing up, Liz looked one last time at the old tombstone, then joined Tom as he approached the school. "I feel different about the cemetery now. Somehow it makes me feel good."

"Me too."

The school's only lights came from basement windows. Looking into a furnace room, they saw Black Dog staring into the eyes of Mickey Mouse. After a moment Black Dog walked away from the poster of the grinning mouse, and began pounding on some metal with a large mallet. He paused to wipe sweat from his forehead, then again the powerful blows rang out.

"What's he doing?"

Tom shook his head. "I don't know, but look at

the muscles on that guy. He sure doesn't look skinny with his shirt off."

"Should we go home?"

"No. Not when we promised Mrs. Zinck we'd help."

They found a basement door, and waited for the hammering to pause before they knocked. Seconds later they were looking at Black Dog's irritated face. Sweat poured down past his fierce black eyes into the wiry tangles of his beard. "Yeah?"

"Uh," Tom stammered, "uh, hi there, Mr. Dog. We, uh . . ."

"We came for a visit," Liz said, with a big smile. "We're interested in your art."

"I'm busy."

"Can't we come in, just for a minute?"

"No."

Tom put his hand on the heavy metal door as it began to close. "Can we talk about the danger facing Professor Zinck?"

Black Dog stared at Tom for a moment, then stepped aside. "Come in."

They crossed a large room with a concrete floor, which seemed to be a winter play area for the school kids, and followed Black Dog into a brick-walled room with a huge furnace. Wind blasted down the chimney, making a loud *whooooo!*, and then died away for a few seconds before another gust repeated the alarming sound. Along the walls were brooms and mops and dusters, but Tom's eyes instantly spotted a container of *DEATH TO RATS* poison and a pulse throbbed in his throat.

"What's this about Professor Zinck?" Black Dog sprawled in a battered old armchair, with one of his hands dangling close to the mallet on the floor.

Tom searched his mind for the right words. His reckless statement had got them into the school, but what should he say now? "We're afraid for the Zincks," he said at last, watching for Black Dog's reaction. "They face a great danger."

"Why come to me?"

Tom considered mentioning Professor Zinck's will, but knew that wouldn't be fair. "Liz and I will be keeping watch on the Manor. Would you help us?"

The man snorted. "I've got a job to do here, and my art. I admit you've got me concerned for the Zincks, but I don't have time to hang around outside the Manor."

"Then we'll do it alone," Tom said, hoping this would warn Black Dog not to try anything. "We'll be there, night and day."

"*The eye that never sleeps*," Black Dog smirked. "That's the famous motto of the Pinkerton Detective Agency. Are you two in the same racket?"

"Maybe," Tom said, then quickly changed the subject. "How come you've got that poster of Mickey Mouse?"

Reaching for the mallet, Black Dog stood up. "I'm creating my interpretation of the icons of our culture. Do you see this metal sculpture? It shows how I feel about Mickey Mouse, Charlie Brown and Elvis Presley." With a savage swing, he brought the mallet crashing down on the metal. The room echoed with the blow, then it was repeated with even more force, making Tom and Liz cover their ears.

"What have you got against those guys?" Tom shouted.

Black Dog's laugh was sudden and unexpected. "Nothing! Can't you tell that this sculpture praises them?"

"No, I sure can't."

Again, the deep laugh. "Well, you're honest. I like that." He seemed to have relaxed, and Liz spoke up before he could swing the mallet again.

"How old is this school, Mr. Dog?"

"Listen, kid, that's not my real name. It's Arthur Brown, but I call myself Black Dog because it sounds more interesting. This place was opened in 1895."

"Wow! Our school in Winnipeg isn't nearly that old. Would you show us around?"

"O.K., but only if you promise to leave me in peace afterwards."

Putting down the mallet, he led them to a wooden staircase which creaked underfoot. They reached a hallway where the hardwood floors shone under a thick coat of wax, and pipes crossed the ceiling in crooked patterns. Looking into a classroom, Tom was surprised to find it bright and cheerful.

"Hey, this place isn't bad. They've got normal desks and boards, and nice pictures up on the walls. And look, Liz, you're featured on that list of French words!"

"Where?"

"Can't you see it says *la banane*?"

"Funny man," Liz said, annoyed because Black Dog had laughed. "It also describes Tom Austen as *le pain*, meaning he is le-pain-in-le-neck."

Black Dog walked down the hallway. "You want to see the next floor? It's condemned as a fire hazard." His footsteps echoed as they went up the enclosed staircase into musty darkness. When he switched on a light, Tom and Liz were surprised to find themselves under the gaze of a magnificent eagle. Beside it in a display case they saw a dusty albatross, a hermit crab, and a snake with its red tongue sticking out.

Desks and old textbooks were stacked beside the display case. Every word echoed in this empty space, and the windows rattled in the wind. The school made Tom think of movies in which people were held prisoner in attic rooms.

"Is there an attic?" he asked, hoping the answer would be no.

"Right up there." Black Dog pointed at some narrow steel stairs. "From the attic you can get outside, and cross the roof to the bell tower." Turning, he stared at Tom. "But that wind would blow you right off the roof."

"Don't worry, I'm not going to try it."

Liz poked her head into a storeroom, where a moth-eaten Red Ensign hung on the wall. "Hey, look at that fancy telescope!"

"Leave it alone!" Black Dog said sharply, as Liz walked over to the telescope. "That's mine, and it's very delicate."

"I'm sorry," Liz said, blushing. She turned to

the storeroom's small oval window and looked at the cemetery far below, its trees bending under the wind. "This room must have an incredible view on a clear day."

Black Dog mumbled a reply and headed for the stairs. Clearly the tour, and the conversation, had reached an end. Black Dog said nothing more, and within minutes Tom and Liz were standing outside the school in the thick fog, with night rapidly falling.

"Well," Liz said, "that was a dud investigation. We didn't learn a thing."

"No, but we scared Black Dog. He knows we're wise to his game." Tom pointed at the light which streamed into the foggy darkness from the furnace-room window. "Let's watch him for a while. He may panic, and try to get back to the Professor."

Keeping back from the window, they had a good view of Black Dog. For a few minutes the man pounded on his metal sculpture, but then he put down the mallet and began pacing the floor. Suddenly he reached for a switch and the room went black.

Tom and Liz scrambled into hiding behind a tree and lay listening to the mournful cry of a foghorn somewhere in the night. What was Black Dog doing? Within seconds the basement door screeched on its hinges, then a lean figure stepped out of the school and hurried away into the fog.

"After him!" Tom whispered urgently.

Stumbling past the tombstones, they managed

to keep Black Dog in sight only because he passed under a streetlight before heading toward a row of elegant old houses.

"He must be going to the Manor!"

"Those legs of his move so fast, we'll never keep up."

"We've got to!"

For a few minutes it seemed as if they had lost Black Dog. Then they caught sight of him in the long shaft of light coming from the window of a church. Quickly he returned to darkness, and his footsteps died away.

Hurrying past the church, Tom pointed at a narrow street. "He went along there."

"No, I'm sure he walked straight down the hill."

Tom tried to see through the night, but it was impossible. The fog gripped the town, muffling every sound and hiding everything except the feeble glow of lights from porches and windows. Black Dog was gone.

"We must get to the Manor!"

"But where is it?"

"Somewhere around here. This street, maybe, or the next."

Eventually they found Lunenburg Manor, but not before precious time had been lost. A single light was visible in the tower, but no one answered their urgent knocking. Finally Liz tried the door, and it opened.

"What should we do?" she whispered.

"We'd better get up to the Professor's bedroom and see if he's O.K."

The house was in total silence. As Tom and Liz climbed the tower stairs the foghorn sounded, far away and sorrowful, but they heard nothing else until they reached the long upper hallway. Then they heard the low whining of Boss, followed by the creaking of floorboards.

The Professor's door opened. Dancing light from the fireplace showed Boss lying in the hallway, then a thin man with blond hair came out of the bedroom and closed the door. After being visible for a moment in the hallway's dim light, he disappeared through the shadows toward the service stairs.

"Who was that?" Tom said.

"Not so loud! He might hear you."

Boss continued to whine as they tip-toed along the hallway to Professor Zinck's room. Inside, the coal fire burned silently, making strange patterns of light on the walls. Dark shadows hid the Professor's face as Tom and Liz went cautiously to the bed.

"Oh no!" Liz said, leaning forward. "He's dead!"

"Impossible!"

Tom went closer, and stared in horror at the Professor. For a moment he felt faint, then tears ran down his cheeks. "I don't believe it. He was our friend."

Liz was crying. The firelight glistened on her wet face as she walked away from the bed, trying to control her sobbing. She stood in the middle of the room with her head bowed, then suddenly knelt down. "Tom. Look at this."

"What is it?"

Liz held up a small bottle. "This is for insulin. Why is it here?"

"I don't know. Professor Zinck didn't use insulin."

Liz returned to the bed. "There's a pin-prick of blood on his arm from a needle. The Professor *has* been murdered, Tom. Someone gave him an overdose of insulin."

"It was that blond man! We'd better phone the police."

A footstep sounded behind them, followed by a *phssssst* as gas was released from a capsule. There was no smell, but suddenly Tom's nose and throat were on fire. He sank to his knees, struggling to breathe, then saw yellow bombs exploding inside his eyes. Next came darkness, as smooth and luxurious as velvet.

# 6

Thunder awakened Tom.

He was aware of cramps in his stomach, and all his body ached. Even the muscles of his eyes were stiff as he opened them and looked around a small room.

Liz was asleep on another bed. Using some water, Tom managed to get her awake, and they went outside. Above the door, a sign said *Rest Easy Cottage*.

"What's that noise?" Liz mumbled, still half-asleep.

"I think it's thunder, but there's no rain."

"Where are we?"

"Some kind of resort. There's other cottages, and some picnic tables. We'd better find the office."

A woman looked up with a smile as they entered the office. "You're awake early. Are you the new kids in *Rest Easy Cottage*?"

"We're . . ."

"Your father forgot to sign the register last night. Would you ask him to stop by?"

"Our parents are in Winnipeg," Liz said. "That man who posed as our father may be a killer."

The woman smiled. "And I may be Cinderella."

Tom leaned over the counter. "We're serious! Last night Professor Zinck was murdered, and we think his killer is the man who brought us here."

"Did you say Professor Zinck? But, I know him. He can't be dead!"

"It's true! Can you tell us where to find the police?"

Instead of answering, the woman walked slowly to the window and stood looking out. "I can't believe it. He was such a good man, and so kind to people."

"Is the police station close by? We're anxious to get there."

She turned to them with sad eyes. "The police are in Lunenburg, which is too far to walk. I'll phone them and say we're coming. We'll drive down as soon as my assistant gets to work."

"If this isn't Lunenburg, where are we?"

"You're at the Ovens."

"What's that?"

The woman looked at her watch. "Go outside, and follow the signs. Be back here in thirty minutes. Then we'll be able to leave."

Outside the office, Liz started crying. "The Professor's dead, Tom. I don't want to look at some stupid ovens."

"We might as well. We can't leave yet."

"He knew he was going to die," Liz whispered, shivering. "Remember his forerunner?"

"We've *got* to find that blond person!"

"He must be the man who put us under with knock-out gas and then brought us here. But why?"

The thunder grew louder as they went through the woods to the top of a cliff. Dark clouds lay over the sea, and a strong wind drove white waves in toward the cliff. From below came the constant booming of thunder.

"Look, Tom, there are caves all along the bottom of the cliff. The thunder's coming from the caves."

"Maybe we can get down to them."

Following a path along the cliff, they came to a sign reading *Cannon Cave*. Steps had been built into the cliff, and Tom and Liz cautiously followed these down to the interior of a cave, where a platform looked down on seething green water rushing in from the sea. Jagged rocks hung from the cave roof like sharp teeth, and the thunder came in deafening claps.

"I see what causes it!" Liz shouted above the noise. "Watch what happens when a wave jams through that hole in the back of the cave."

Tom watched the next wave surge into the cave. The green water was squeezed between the narrow rocky walls, then forced its way through a hole into a small cavern. After a moment's pause, there was a terrible BOOM as the wave smashed into the walls of the cavern.

Foam and white water hissed out of the hole, followed by a blast of wind that tore at their bodies. "It's almost strong enough to knock us into the water!" Tom shouted. "This place could be a death trap."

"Especially if a wave swept us through that hole. We'd be squished to death."

"Let's get going! I've seen enough."

At the top of the cliff, pausing to rest from the climb, they watched a trawler heading out to sea. "It's coming from Lunenburg," Tom said. "I remember noticing the caves along this cliff when Cap'n John took us to Oak Island."

"How do we get back to the office? There's more than one path."

"I think it's this way."

But, instead of leading to the office, the path wound through the woods to a grassy hill overlooking a cove. As they gazed down at surf pounding on a rocky beach, Liz grabbed Tom's arm.

"Look! There's Black Dog!"

The man sat on a beached motorboat at the far end of the cove, staring at the big waves. A tote bag was at his feet, and his hair looked wet, but there was no apparent reason for him being there.

"What should we do, Liz?"

"I don't know. It's your case."

"Black Dog scares me, especially now that the Professor's been murdered. He may be partners with that blond killer."

"Let's go question him. If he really is involved with the murder, we'll soon know."

"Do you think it's safe?"

"Sure. He can't hurt us, not in broad daylight."

Black Dog's eyes never left the waves, even as Tom and Liz approached him along the rocky beach. He seemed deep in thought, but finally looked up after Tom coughed noisily.

"What are you kids doing here?"

"We don't know. Maybe you've got a blond friend who can tell us."

Ignoring the anger in Liz's voice, Black Dog watched spray fly from a big wave as it smashed down on the rocks. "Get lost."

"Sure we'll go. Straight to the police."

"What for?"

"Stop acting innocent! The Professor's been murdered, and we're going to tell the police everything we know."

Black Dog frowned. "What did you say?"

"We know it was murder, and we know about the insulin."

"The Professor is *dead*?"

"You're a good actor," Liz said scornfully. "Maybe the police will give you an Oscar, or maybe a life sentence."

"The fools!" Black Dog slammed his fist against the boat. "I warned them!"

Seizing the tote bag, he broke into a run. Tom went after him, but his feet slipped on the rocks, and he couldn't keep up with Black Dog's long-legged run. The man disappeared into the woods, and Tom waited unhappily for Liz to join him.

"I guess we blew it, letting Black Dog escape like that. We should have called in the police to arrest him."

"On what evidence?"

Tom shrugged. "He looks guilty, and he acts guilty."

"We'll need a lot more than that. I wonder if he really has got a blond friend?"

Tom's eyes lit up. "Or maybe a blond wig!"

Liz snapped her fingers. "Good thinking. We'd better tell the police that the killer could have been someone wearing a blond wig."

"Should we tell them about Black Dog?"

"They won't listen. Not without any proof. We'll have to watch him ourselves, and see if he makes a slip."

Shortly after, they reached the Lunenburg police station and were astonished by the uproar their arrival caused. Then they realized they'd been missing all night. After telling the police what had happened, they learned that Professor Zinck's death was thought to have been caused by a heart attack, but the coroner would now check for an insulin overdose.

The Gouldens were called and they quickly arrived at the police station, relieved that Tom and Liz were safe. Then Carl stated, in very clear language, that their detective work was over.

"But what about the Professor?" Tom protested. "Don't you want his killer found?"

Shirley nodded. "Of course. We're terribly upset about the Professor's death, but I'm sure the police will find the person responsible."

76

"The police? They thought Professor Zinck had died of a heart attack!"

"Now, Tom . . ."

"I'm sorry," he muttered. "I just wish we could have a chance to break this case."

"Forget it, Tom, or your vacation will be ruined."

"Impossible, not when there's a murder to investigate."

Liz nodded her agreement, and Tom knew she wasn't ready to give up the case either. Back at Stonehurst they met secretly, and agreed that *somehow* they would return to Lunenburg the next day, if only to make sure that Mrs. Zinck was safe.

Still feeling upset about the Professor, Tom went to bed early. Just as he was falling asleep, he felt icy fingers brush against his neck.

Leaping out of bed, he looked out the window just in time to see a shadowy figure slip away through the trees. Then something on the ground caught his eye. Looking down, Tom saw an ice cube.

*An ice cube?* Suddenly part of the puzzle was explained, and Tom returned to bed feeling a whole lot better.

* * *

A hand shook Tom awake. "It's 5 a.m." Carl said. "Time to go fishing."

Tom groaned and tucked his head further under the covers. Then he remembered how he and Liz had begged Carl to take them fishing, and how they'd promised to get up at 5 a.m. without any complaints. Finally he crawled out of bed, pulled on his clothes, and went yawning to the kitchen.

Carl smiled from the stove, where he was pouring mugs of steaming tea. Liz and Wade were at the table, eating toast piled with jam. From somewhere in the house came the sounds of heavy snoring.

"Who's that?"

Wade laughed. "It's Roger Eliot-Stanton. Isn't it gross?"

"Who is that guy, anyway? Why's he here, just hanging around? Doesn't he work for a living? I'd like to check him out."

Carl gave Tom a warning look. "Don't you remember what I said yesterday about giving up detective work?"

"I guess so," Tom muttered.

"Let's concentrate on the fishing. There's a beautiful night outside. The weather should be fine."

Tom hoped good weather meant the sea would be calm. Everyone had predicted that he and Liz would be seasick, and he wanted to prove them wrong. Even so, he couldn't help studying the *Mariner's Prayer* on the wall:

*O, God*
*Thy sea is so great*
*And my boat is so small*

They walked to the wharf past sleeping houses and stacks of lobster traps. Although it still seemed

78

like the middle of the night, the waterfront was alive with activity. Even the seagulls were wide awake, wheeling and screaming above the little boats as they headed out to sea, their path through the darkness marked only by red and green running-lights and the low growl of their engines.

Carl and Wade stopped beside some other fishermen to discuss weather conditions, while Tom and Liz walked on to the wharf. The moon had faded to pale white, shining above a lighthouse on the rocky shore.

"I hope Mrs. Zinck is O.K.," Liz said. "I've been thinking about her all night."

"We should go and see her soon, to be sure she's safe. I want to tell her how awful I feel about Professor Zinck dying."

"Carl and Shirley are driving to Lunenburg tonight. We could get a ride from them."

"Good idea. They can't object to us visiting Mrs. Zinck."

"Let's hope not." Liz looked at the pink light creeping into the eastern sky, and a stray gust of wind tossed her black hair. "Going to be seasick?"

"No way . . . I hope."

Soon they were roaring out to sea in the gill-netter, leaving a deep wake behind. Tom and Liz sat in the stern, a chilly wind on their faces, and watched Carl and Wade prepare a net with expert fingers. After leaving the harbour mouth, which was marked by a big rock covered with seagulls and hammered by waves, they headed into rougher seas. For a few minutes Tom thought he would be sick, then his body began adjusting to the swells and he learned to anticipate the cold water spraying back from the bow.

"When's lunch?" he asked, delighted that he'd be able to eat it.

Carl laughed. "About seven hours from now."

"Brother!"

Tom looked at Liz in dismay, wondering how he would survive the boredom. But soon the action began in earnest, with Carl and Wade hauling up a long net from the sea bed and working quickly to untangle each fish.

"What kind are those?"

"Haddock," Wade answered, throwing one into a wooden crate on the deck. "Watch them come up through the water in the net. They look all silvery."

Liz leaned close to look at the fish, then smiled at Wade. "You must really like it out here."

"I do. It feels good sharing the work with Dad, and learning about the sea from him."

Tom couldn't help envying Wade's skill as a fisherman, and admiring his bravery in facing the open sea. "Doesn't it scare you?" he asked. "Being so far out here, in this tiny boat?"

"Sometimes," Carl said. "I've been fishing for a quantity of years, and lost some good friends. They're gone from life so suddenly, you understand. Already this year eight men and women have drowned from their boats along this coast."

"It sounds awful."

"Sure it is, but those who survive the terrible

storms and certain death, why, they change. Somehow they're stronger and prouder, for what they've overcome."

"Shouldn't you quit while you're still ahead?" Liz asked.

Carl shook his head. "Not the way I love this sea. You should be out here when the whales are mating. They leap clear out of the waves and make rainbows in the air."

"Have you ever seen a shark?"

"Lots of blue sharks here in summer. Some fellows brought one on board from their net, thinking it was dead. But it woke up fast, and slashed off Ben's arm. He screamed all the way to the hospital. Six hours, just screaming."

"How horrible." Feeling sick, Tom scanned the waves, searching for the deadly fin that could be slicing their way at this moment. "About what time do we go home?"

Wade grinned. "Thinking about sharks, Tom?"

"Of course not. I just don't want to miss the soap operas this afternoon."

"I hear there's a new one called *As Tom's Stomach Turns*. Our hero is out on a gillnetter, and starts barfing when he notices the boat is always rising and falling, rising and falling, rising . . ."

For a ghastly moment, Tom felt his breakfast coming up as Wade's hypnotic voice droned on. Then the crisis passed, and Carl straightened up from the net, rubbing his back. "Weather's changing. We'll haul one more net, then head for in. I'd say there's a heavy nor'easter coming on."

Liz studied the cloudless sky. "How can you tell it's changing?"

Wade smiled proudly. "Dad's been fishing since he was fourteen. Not much he can't tell you about weather and tides and currents. He's a real Bluenoser."

"What's that mean, anyway? Everyone in Nova Scotia talks about Bluenosers."

Carl laughed. "If you came out fishing in December you'd soon be one yourself. It's so cold on the sea that fishermen's noses turn blue."

"So that's it!" Liz watched the last of the fish land in the crate with a wet squelch.

"Now, let's have a mug-up." Carl opened a Thermos, then passed around haddock sandwiches. "These are some good," he said, biting into one. "You two heard about Devil's Island?"

"No, sir."

"Well, it seems the government owns a nice little house on Devil's Island, and anyone can have it for free. But there's nobody yet who's tried it and stayed. They say a fisherman lived there long ago. His wife and six kids died in a fire while he was out in his boat, and now his ghost roams the island looking for them."

"Dad's got some great ghost stories," Wade said, grinning. "Say, Tom, when are you going to investigate the ghost of the *Young Teazer*? Everyone in Stonehurst is waiting for your solution."

"Don't worry, Wade. I haven't forgotten."

The snack was over too quickly, and they headed for a fluorescent buoy which marked another of the nets. As he helped haul it up, Wade untangled an ugly brown fish and threw it on the deck beside Tom. Blowing angrily through its mouth, the fish stared at him with eyes that bulged from two bumps on its head.

"That's a sculpin. A gang of bikers was out here, and took one home to mount on their clubhouse wall." Wade picked up the fish to look at its warted body and the horns growing out of its head, then threw it overboard. "Man, that thing is evil-looking."

*Evil*. Tom's mind flashed back to Oak Island, where Professor Zinck had written EVEL after being attacked. If only they'd worked out that clue, perhaps the Professor would be alive today.

"Maybe it's part of someone's name. Or a set of initials."

Liz glanced at Tom. "Talking in your sleep?"

"What did EVEL mean, Liz? And what about the Professor's car keys? I'm sure we've missed an important clue in that."

"You know what upsets me? I have a sickening feeling that another person's life is threatened, and yet we can't do anything. And I'm sure the killer is someone we know."

As the gillnetter headed for port Tom thought about each person he'd met since arriving in Nova Scotia, and how each could benefit by the death of Professor Zinck. Possibilities tumbled inside his head, as plentiful as the seagulls which tumbled and shrieked behind the boat, fighting for the scraps that Carl and Wade threw overboard as they dressed the haddock.

"You were right about the weather," Liz said from the wheel, which she'd asked to try. "Those are mean-looking clouds on the horizon."

"Yup," Carl said. "It's breezing up some."

Breeze is hardly the word, Tom thought, as a wind slammed in from sea just after they reached port, making the gillnetters dance at anchor and pounding the rocks with huge breakers. They hurried home, getting there just as the first rain blew around their heads.

"Were you seasick?" Holli asked immediately.

Carla turned from the piano. "I bet they were!"

Wade sprawled on the sofa, grinning. "I've never seen such a green face. Why, we only just put to sea and . . ."

"And Tom was just fine," Carl said from the kitchen. "Now, Wade, I have something to discuss with you."

The grin dissolved. "What is it, Dad?"

"Charlie Oxner says he caught you loading a raft with wood last night. Were you planning to set it on fire, and float it across the harbour?"

"Well, um . . ."

"Answer me!"

Wade lowered his head. "Yes, I guess I was."

"So that 'ghost ship' we saw the other night was just a burning raft?"

"Yes, Dad."

"Floated across the harbour by you?"

Wade nodded, his eyes on the floor. "Am I in trouble?"

"You can bet on that. When your mother gets home we'll discuss your punishment. For now, you can go to your room."

As Wade left, Tom smiled happily. So the ghost ship had only been a prank arranged by Wade. The gag had fallen on its face, but there was another score to settle. Just be patient, he told himself, and Wade will truly *suffer*.

After getting a handful of blueberries from the kitchen, Tom sat on the sofa to listen while Carla sang hymns. It felt good to have survived the fishing trip, especially when Shirley returned from Lunenburg and also wanted to know if they'd been seasick.

The only person who didn't ask was Roger Eliot-Stanton, who came out of his room shortly after. He surprised everyone by complimenting Carla on her singing, then sat down beside Tom with a book.

Tom shifted away, and continued reading a newspaper article headlined *Tragic Death of Professor Carol Zinck*. "It doesn't say anything about an insulin overdose. Maybe the police are keeping that quiet, to avoid alerting the killer."

Roger Eliot-Stanton's eyebrows rose in a thin line. "What's this about an insulin overdose?"

Tom hid his face behind the newspaper. "Nothing," he mumbled, furious that he'd revealed secret information.

"The police suspect insulin killed Professor Zinck?"

"Who can say?"

Tom's face remained hidden until he'd stopped blushing. Even then, he didn't begin feeling better about his mistake until he'd gorged on a big meal of chili and homemade brown bread, followed by a bowl of blueberries, huckleberries and blackberries smothered in whipped cream. Somehow the food made him feel good, even about facing the Manor on such a stormy night.

As they drove into Lunenburg, Shirley looked carefully at Tom and Liz. "You're only planning to visit Mrs. Zinck?"

"Yes."

"No detective work?"

"You can count on us."

"That's not an answer." A blast of wind shook the car and thunder crackled. "We don't want another search party, especially on a night like this."

"No need to worry about us," Tom said, as the car pulled up in front of Lunenburg Manor.

"I'm not convinced," Carl commented, watching Tom and Liz get out into the storm. "Now, don't be late meeting us."

"No sweat!" Liz said cheerfully. "We'll be perfectly safe."

"Let's hope so," Tom murmured, looking up at the Manor just as lightning flashed across the black sky, its jagged light reflected briefly in the dark windows of the tower. A clap of thunder followed, and cold rain lashed their faces as they ran to the shelter of a big oak in the yard.

"I think the power's out. No lights are showing."

"Even so, Mrs. Zinck is probably home. Let's go knock."

"The power's out everywhere," Tom said, stalling for time. "I can see candles in those other houses, but not in the Manor."

"You really messed up today, Tom."

"How?"

"By telling Roger Eliot-Stanton about the insulin. What if he's involved in the murder?"

"You're right, it was a dumb mistake." The rain was soaking Tom's clothes, making him feel miserable. "By the way, where is Roger Eliot-Stanton tonight? Did you notice?"

"He went to his room after dinner. But he could be anywhere by now."

"What a thought."

Tom looked up at the Manor, trying to locate Mrs. Zinck's room, then his eyes went to the looming dark shape of the tower. As lightning burst across the sky, Tom suddenly saw the horrifying image of Professor Zinck at a tower window, a silent cry on his lips.

# 7

"Did you see that?" Tom gasped.

"What?"

"I'd swear I just saw the Professor's ghost, haunting this place! Let's get out of here!"

Tom ran. Lightning and thunder exploded above his head, but all he could see was the terrible vision of the Professor's face, crying out. Finally he stopped running and gasped for breath.

"Tom!"

Somewhere in the night, Liz was calling his name. Summoning strength, he returned her shout, and moments later she came out of the darkness.

"You ran like the wind, Tom! I couldn't keep up."

"It was horrible, Liz. I'll never forget that face."

"Do you see where we are?" Liz waited for a

lightning flash, then pointed at a row of wet tombstones. "Look, up beyond the cemetery, some lights are on. How come the school's got power?"

"It must have its own generator. Let's go see Black Dog."

"What? Are you crazy?"

"Liz, we've got to do *something*, and Black Dog is our only real suspect."

"You're going to see him now? On a night like this?"

"That's right," Tom turned toward the cemetery. "Coming?"

"What'll you say to him?"

"I don't know, Liz, but I have this awful feeling that Mrs. Zinck is in real danger. We *must* grill Black Dog and force him to make a slip. Then the police can arrest him, and Mrs. Zinck will be safe."

Liz looked at the trees bending low under the wind which shrieked across the hilltop. "I don't like it."

"Wait here, then." Tom went into the cemetery, trying not to notice the branches clattering above the dim shapes of the tombstones. He wished desperately that Liz would come too, but he wasn't going to ask her again.

"Tom! Wait for me."

With a sigh of relief, he stopped. "I thought you weren't coming!"

"First I had to count slowly to ten for good luck."

"We may need it."

Together they went through the cemetery, doubled over against the wind. The lights from the school beckoned them on, but before they could reach it Liz seized Tom's arm.

"Listen! Did you hear that?"

"What?"

"Three slow taps. That's our forerunner, Tom!"

Liz's eyes were wide with fright, and Tom's own heart was pounding wildly. Then he saw two swings in the school's playground, slapping against each other in the wind. "There's the tapping," he said. "You see, we're not about to die."

Liz tried to smile, and Tom led the way to the school's basement door, but there was no answer to his knock. Opening the door, he called Black Dog's name but got no reply. They tip-toed toward the furnace room, casting anxious glances at the shadowed corners. "Black Dog's not going to leap out at us." Tom said with a feeble laugh. "He's probably upstairs, cleaning the boards or something."

"My heart's in overdrive. It may never recover."

With a sudden *whooooo!* the wind blasted down the furnace chimney, making them jump. Mickey Mouse was still on the wall, waving a white-gloved hand, but where was Black Dog?

Upstairs, they went through the hallways calling his name and nervously checking each classroom. But they were all empty, which left only the condemned floor above.

"Why are we doing this?" Liz said. "We're supposed to be at the Manor, protecting Mrs. Zinck."

"We can't quit now. Besides, Black Dog's our major suspect. He's the only one we know of who's got anything to gain by the Professor's death."

Arriving on the top floor, they were greeted by a lizard which grinned wickedly from a display case. There were still old desks and stacks of dusty texts, and the windows still rattled and banged in the wind, but this time there was no Black Dog to stop Liz from examining the telescope.

"It's trained on the harbour. This thing is so strong, I can practically read the boat names when the lightning flashes."

Tom went to her side, and stood looking down at the cemetery far below. For some reason he remembered the graves of the twin boys, and the discussion that had followed.

"Hey!" Liz exclaimed. "I think I just saw Mrs. Zinck."

"Impossible."

"I can see a skiff with a motor, heading out toward the boats in the harbour. There are two people in it, all bundled up, and I'm pretty sure Mrs. Zinck is one of them."

"Let me see."

Tom squinted into the telescope, and was surprised at its strength. Even spray could be seen, flying over the boats which strained against their anchor cables. Shifting the telescope slightly, he saw a skiff disappearing behind a boat which heaved in the stormy seas.

"I just missed seeing who's in that skiff. But do you want to know something weird? I think those people are aiming to get aboard Cap'n John's boat."

"What can that mean?"

"I don't know, but it makes me feel nervous. If someone *is* after the Professor's money, they may want to get rid of Mrs. Zinck, too. What should we do?"

"I'm not absolutely positive it was Mrs. Zinck in the skiff, so let's find out if she's at the Manor. If not, we'll have to call the police."

"I just hope she's O.K.!"

They raced downstairs and out of the school. The rest of the town remained in darkness, and they stumbled down several wrong streets before they realized they were lost. Liz went to a house and got directions, but these proved to be wrong. Then they learned from another house that Lunenburg Manor was ten blocks away. Finally Tom and Liz reached it, wet and exhausted and very frightened for Mrs. Zinck.

Trying not to think about what he'd seen in the tower window, Tom knocked on the door. Eventually it swung open, revealing Henneyberry's sad face.

"Yes?"

"Mr. Henneyberry, please let us in. We're really worried about Mrs. Zinck."

"But she's asleep."

"We've *got* to see her! Otherwise we'll have to ask the police to make sure she's safe."

"Very well, then. If you are that upset."

Henneyberry stepped aside and they went into the hallway, where a single candle flickered on a table and the air was filled with groans and creaks.

Liz looked at Henneyberry. "When did you last actually *see* Mrs. Zinck?"

"Earlier this evening. Perhaps two hours ago, just before the power failed."

"So she's been unprotected since then?"

This suggestion seemed to annoy Henneyberry. "I haven't left the Manor all day, in case she needed me."

"But what about the service stairs in the back, Mr. Henneyberry? Could someone have crept up those stairs to her room without you knowing?"

"It's possible." Henneyberry gazed at Tom and Liz, no doubt wondering why they were so upset. But then he managed a smile. "All right. Since it's so important to you, you can see Mrs. Zinck."

"Terrific!" Tom said, starting for the stairs.

"Just a minute. Let me go up first. She'll want to awaken properly before seeing you."

"I guess you're right." Tom tried to hide his impatience as Henneyberry picked up the candle, then put it down and went slowly to a closet. "Excuse me, sir, but what are you doing?"

"The hallway upstairs is drafty, so the candle could blow out. I'll need to use a storm lantern."

Moving at a maddening crawl, Henneyberry opened the closet door, looked up at the shelves to locate the storm lantern, then went along the hallway to get a small velvet chair. Returning to the closet, he climbed on the chair to reach the lantern, then got carefully down and took the chair back to its former place. Finally, after dusting the storm lantern and searching his pockets for matches, he got the lantern burning and plodded up the stairs.

During all this time Tom paced the floor, trying not to worry about Mrs. Zinck and desperately fighting thoughts of the Professor's ghost. Finally he flung himself down on the velvet chair, but the seat was wet and he returned to his pacing.

"He's taking so long, Liz! I'm going *mental*!"

"Let's go upstairs."

Holding the candle that Henneyberry had left, Liz started up the tower stairs. Without warning, a bolt of lightning lit up the stained-glass windows, then thunder crackled across the sky. Rain rattled against the windows as the Manor groaned under the storm's attack.

Reaching the top floor, they found no sign of Henneyberry. "This is where Mrs. Zinck has her bedroom," Liz said. "Why can't we see the light from the storm lantern?"

A sudden draft gusted down the hallway, blowing out the candle. Total darkness surrounded them, and Tom's heart beat fearfully as he thought about Mrs. Zinck.

"I'm sure she's out in Cap'n John's boat. Let's get out of here, and go tell the police. This place freaks me!"

The black air and the groaning of the Manor were almost more than Tom could stand, and he crashed down the stairs in a near panic with Liz right behind, her breathing harsh and frightened. A light came from below, and Tom cried out in alarm as they rounded the final bend in the staircase and stumbled to a halt.

The man with thick blond hair was waiting for them in the hallway below, one hand covering his mouth and nose with a wet cloth. He held up a capsule and there was a *phssssst* of escaping gas. As fire filled Tom's throat, he stared into the man's eyes.

"It's you!" he gasped, before he slid into darkness.

# 8

Tom's body tumbled one way until it struck wood,
then flopped back against metal. Creaks and rat-
tles filled his ears, and there was a rushing sound
he couldn't identify.

He opened his eyes and saw Professor Zinck
lying nearby. An engine thudded somewhere near
Tom's head, filling the air with fumes. As Tom
slowly woke up, he realized that he was inside
Cap'n John's tour boat, which was fighting its
way through heavy seas. Waves rushed past outside the wooden hull, and occasionally Tom's

body was lifted into the air as the storm slammed into the boat.

Tom flexed his aching muscles, then slowly sat up. The big engine pounded in the middle of the cabin. Slumped on a bench near it were Liz and Mrs. Zinck, both staring unhappily at the man at the wheel.

Henneyberry.

The blond wig made him look ridiculous, but the pistol tucked into his belt made him look deadly. Tom's eyes went to Henneyberry's feet, which were soaking wet from the rain. Then he remembered the wet velvet chair at the Manor. Henneyberry had lied when he claimed to have been indoors all day, since his feet had soaked the chair.

Where was the man taking them? The rain-lashed darkness outside the windows gave no clue, and Henneyberry was silent as he concentrated on the boat's struggle through the stormy seas.

As Tom glanced at Professor Zinck lying on the deck, his heart leapt in terror. The Professor's eyes had flickered.

There was no further movement, and Tom was sure Henneyberry's knock-out gas was still playing tricks with his brain. Then a giant wave smashed against the boat, rolling it to one side. As Tom struggled for balance, he saw the Professor open his eyes.

Mrs. Zinck cried out, and stumbled to her husband's side. "You're alive! It can't be possible, but you're alive!"

97

Professor Zinck mumbled a reply, then shook his head and managed to sit up. He kissed and hugged his wife with tenderness, but when his eyes turned to Henneyberry they burned with rage.

"You'll pay for this, Henneyberry."

The man laughed. "Say your prayers, Professor. You and your missus aren't long for this world."

"Don't be a fool. You won't get away with it."

Henneyberry smiled, then twisted the wheel to take the boat straight into a towering wave. Tom was thrown against the hull, and then tumbled across the deck toward Henneyberry's feet. Looking up, he saw the pistol in the man's belt. Could he reach it?

Liz seemed to read Tom's mind, for she distracted Henneyberry with a question. "How can Professor Zinck be alive, when we saw him dead?"

"Very simple. The man who died was the Professor's twin brother, Evelyn."

"I should have known!"

"A while ago Evelyn came to me with a plan for getting the Professor's money, and I agreed to help in return for a large cash payment. The first step was to attack Professor Zinck when he was away from the Manor, so his wife couldn't interfere."

"So you waited for our trip to Oak Island?"

"Yes. After the attack we hid him in that abandoned car until no one was around, then returned him to Lunenburg by boat and kept him prisoner in the Manor's tower. Meanwhile, Evelyn pretended to be the Professor."

"So that's why both Mrs. Zinck and Boss were afraid of him."

Sea water crashed over the boat, forcing Henneyberry to battle the wheel, but he was back in control before Tom could find the courage to grab the pistol.

"Then came part two of our plan," said Henneyberry, apparently not guessing why Tom remained so close to his feet. "The lawyer was summoned, and the will changed to leave everything to the Professor's brother. Now all the money would be his, but only if Professor and Mrs. Zinck could die in an unfortunate accident."

"Which you were going to arrange?"

Henneyberry nodded. "Then Evelyn got cold feet. He was upset at the thought of murdering his brother and Mrs. Zinck, and finally decided to tell the police what we'd done. That would have meant a long prison sentence, for kidnapping the Professor."

"But surely that's better than murdering someone!"

"You forget, I'm an old man. If I'd gone to prison for kidnapping, I'd have died there. So I tried to convince Evelyn to continue with the original plan. When he refused, I killed him with an overdose of insulin."

The words were spoken quietly and without emotion, which shocked Tom. He couldn't understand how the man was able to speak so easily about murdering someone, but he knew that meant he would as easily kill again. Henneyberry had to be stopped. Again Tom eyed the gun, and waited his chance.

"So," Henneyberry said with a sigh, "there I was, stuck with the Professor in the tower room. What should I do? Finally I decided that the

Zincks could still have an accident, and I'd slip out of the country with Black Dog's fancy goblet and a few other treasures from the Manor's safe."

"What accident are you talking about?"

He laughed. "You'll know, soon enough. It won't be long before I'll be sailing down the coast to Maine. Cap'n John won't get his boat back, but that can't be helped . . ."

At that moment, an enormous wave crashed broadside into the boat and it reeled over. There was a scream of metal, the lights went out, and frightened cries were heard as everyone was tossed violently through the darkness. Tom's head hit something and for a moment bells rang inside his head, then he opened his eyes. Somehow the boat had righted itself, the lights were back on, and the pistol lay on the deck close by.

As Tom reached for it, a foot came out of nowhere and pinned his wrist to the deck. "No you don't," Henneyberry said, picking up the gun. "No kid is putting me in prison."

"Henneyberry, listen to me." Professor Zinck's voice shook with tension. "Forget this crazy plan, and I'll give you all of our money."

"Sure, and then you'll tell the police I killed your brother. If you hadn't given me such rotten pay, Professor, none of this would be happening. But now you'd better say your prayers."

Henneyberry looked out at the storm. As he did, Liz caught Tom's eye and he realized she had a plan.

"Mr. Henneyberry," he said, trying to keep the man talking, "why did you take us to that cottage at the Ovens?"

"To give myself time to think, and to prepare an alibi. I told the police I'd been out for a long walk, then arrived home to find the Professor dead of a heart attack."

Tom's mind whirled as he tried to think of another question. "Were you the person Liz saw rowing Mrs. Zinck out to this boat?"

"That's right. Then, when I went back to get the Professor, you kids arrived at the Manor. I planned to sneak away and leave you there, but then I heard you talking upstairs about going to the police and I decided I'd better bring you along on this trip. You're such nice kids, it's a shame you have to die."

Tom stared at the man, knowing now that he meant to kill them all. Hopeful that Liz knew how to stop Henneyberry, Tom glanced her way and saw that she was leaning over the engine. Suddenly the thudding stopped, and the engine died into silence with an unhappy hiss. The boat began to wallow dangerously in the waves.

"What happened?" Henneyberry shouted, terror on his face as he looked at the silent engine. "What's wrong with that thing?"

Tom grabbed a bench, and held it tightly as the boat reeled and shuddered, completely at the mercy of the storm. Desperately he prayed that Liz knew what she was doing.

"I guess the engine's not working," she said, raising her voice above the howling wind and the pounding of the waves against the hull.

Henneyberry's face was white as he stared at the engine. "I can't fix it! I don't understand those things."

"I know what's wrong," Liz said.

"Then get it going!"

"First open the cabin door, and throw your gun overboard."

Henneyberry's hands shook as his eyes darted between Liz and the engine. Clearly he knew he was finished without a gun, and yet he feared the storm even more. As he hesitated, the boat lurched and groaned, then rolled almost onto its side. When it righted itself, Henneyberry staggered through the cabin and grabbed the door handle. He took the gun from his belt, then faltered.

"Do it!" Professor Zinck shouted. "Otherwise you'll die with the rest of us!"

Henneyberry pulled open the door. Spray and rain lashed his face, and from somewhere close by came the unbelievable roar of constant thunder. As the gun went overboard and Henneyberry slammed the door, Mrs. Zinck trembled in fear.

"It's the Ovens! That's what he planned for us."

"Start the engine!" Henneyberry screamed at Liz, his voice terror-stricken. "We're almost into the Ovens!"

Another wave pitched the boat onto its side, and Liz had to grab for support as she struggled to fit the distributor cap back into place. Every eye was on her while the boat reeled under each blow from the storm, and the thundering roar grew louder.

"There!" Liz said in relief, as the engine came alive. "We're safe now!"

Henneyberry stumbled forward, grabbed the wheel and got the boat back under control. Open-

102

ing a drawer, he lifted out a revolver and turned with a smile.

"Luckily I brought along a second gun," he said, pointing it at Liz. "Now get away from that engine!"

Tom tried desperately to think of another means of escape as he watched Henneyberry head the boat into the waves and then lock the wheel in place. Waving the gun with ugly menace, Henneyberry gestured at the Zincks to stand up.

"You're going for a little trip into the Ovens."

"Give us a chance, Henneyberry. Please!"

"Get out on the back deck. You kids go with them."

The Zincks reached for each other's hands, and went together onto the stormy deck. Tom blundered slowly through the cabin, hoping that he could somehow knock Henneyberry down or grab the revolver, but there was no opportunity before he reached the deck.

The roar of thunder from the Ovens was like the constant blasting of huge guns. This sound, combined with the shrieking wind, convinced Tom that the end had come.

A spotlight shone from the roof of the boat, gleaming on Professor Zinck's face as he turned to shout something at Henneyberry. Tom couldn't tell whether this was a final plea for mercy, or a cry of hatred, as the wind tore the words from the Professor's mouth and sent them whirling into the darkness.

Henneyberry also shouted without being heard, and gestured at the skiff on the deck. The Zincks seemed finally to accept that Henneyberry would show no mercy, and with brave faces they lifted the skiff over the railing. As it tossed on the sea they climbed down into the little boat, and again reached for each other's hands.

With his gun, Henneyberry waved Liz across the deck toward the skiff. At that moment, the spotlight's glow was cut as something black slithered along the cabin roof and plunged toward Henneyberry.

"No!" he screamed, his anguished cry rising above the storm. Vainly he struggled to free himself from the black shape, then screamed again.

Liz seized Tom's arm and pointed in the direction of the skiff. "It's broken free!"

Whirling around, he saw the skiff drifting away into the darkness. The terrified Zincks were waving and shouting, but their words could not be heard over the roar of the Ovens.

"Climb to the cabin roof!" Liz yelled. "Keep the spotlight on the skiff, and I'll try to steer the boat that way!"

With icy fingers, Tom seized the ladder mounted outside the cabin and struggled up to the roof. Head down against the rain and spray which stung his body, he crawled toward the spotlight. Grabbing its handle, he swung it around and swept the seas in search of the skiff.

The beam picked out a wall of green water surging toward the boat. "No!" Tom cried, then gripped the spotlight as the boat rose over the wave, hung in the air, and slammed back down into the sea. He shook water from his eyes, then watched the spotlight beam travel along the black cliffs and raging surf which marked the location of the deadly Ovens.

Then Tom saw the Zincks, clinging to the skiff as it rose to the crest of a wave and disappeared down into a trough.

"We're coming!" he yelled, even though he knew the Zincks couldn't hear him.

Liz must have seen them too, for the boat turned and battled through the tossing seas in their direction. Tom kept the spotlight trained on the Zincks, trying not to hear the roar of the Ovens.

The boat rose over a foaming green wave and headed straight down toward the skiff. For a terrible moment it seemed as if the two vessels would collide, then suddenly they were alongside each other and the Zincks grabbed the tour boat's railing.

"We did it!" Tom shouted in relief. "They're safe!"

As he shone the spotlight on the rear deck, trying to help the Zincks find their way to safety, a figure dressed completely in black rubber moved forward into the glare and helped Mrs. Zinck over the railing, then did the same for Professor Zinck. When they were both safe, the figure in black turned from the railing into the full glare of the spotlight.

It was Black Dog.

# 9

A few days later, Tom was taking his sixteenth ride on the *Tilt-A-Whirl*, a machine that spun his body and scrambled his brains. "Fantastic," he murmured weakly, as the machine stopped its gyrations and he staggered away.

"Going again?" Liz asked. "You need five more rides to break my record."

"I'm going . . . to be sick." Covering his mouth with both hands, Tom stumbled toward a washroom. Much later, he emerged on shaky legs and saw Liz riding the *Tilt-A-Whirl*, smiling happily as her hair whipped back and forth across her face. Feeling his stomach rise, Tom turned away to stare at the people crowding the midway of the Lunenburg Fisheries Exhibition.

"I guess I win!" Liz grabbed Tom's arm, and hustled him to a food stand which reeked of burnt onions and frying meat. "For my prize I want an oyster-burger and a giant Coke."

"What a combination." Tom shelled out the money for Liz's prize, then closed his eyes as she gobbled the food. "You must have a cast-iron stomach."

Wade Goulden appeared out of the crowd, grinning as usual. "You're looking green, Tom! Did the merry-go-round upset your little tummy?"

"No, but the sight of your mug is spoiling my digestion."

"Too bad you're feeling sick, or I'd challenge you to a lobster-eating contest."

"Any time, Wade, any time."

"By the way, Tom, there's a rumour going around Stonehurst that a certain detective is scared of the dark. Surely it's not true?"

As Wade quickly disappeared into the crowd, Liz shook her head sympathetically. "You should get that guy."

"Don't worry." Tom replied grimly. He pointed at a nearby booth. "Let's go see the scallop-shucking contest."

At the booth, experts with flying fingers swiftly opened and emptied the pretty shells taken from the sea bed. "Look at that judge," Tom whispered, "he's a clone of Roger Eliot-Stanton."

"Imagine two copies of that guy walking around! You know, I still find it hard to believe that Roger Eliot-Stanton is just another tourist visiting Nova Scotia."

"You're right, but what's his story? I've got to know!"

"Maybe he's here for a special contest to pick the Rudest Man in the World." Liz looked at the shifting patterns of adults and children streaming through the Exhibition grounds, then grabbed Tom's arm. "Look! There's Black Dog over at that weight-guessing booth. Let's go say hello!"

Tom shrugged. "O.K., but only because he saved our lives."

"What a hero he was!"

"I still don't understand where he found the strength, when he's got a body like Dietmar Oban. He's so thin, I bet he has to move around in the shower just to get wet."

"Your jokes are a RIOT, Tom. Rotten, Idiotic, Oafish and Tupid."

"Tupid?"

"Yeth. And they thtink, too!"

Laughing, Tom and Liz hurried through the crowd to the booth where a young woman was studying Black Dog in an effort to guess his weight. But, like Tom, she misjudged the man's appearance, and was forced to part with a kewpie doll when her guess was too low.

Seeing Liz, Black Dog smiled and handed her the prize. "Take this home, as a souvenir of your Lunenburg adventure."

Liz gazed at the kewpie doll. "Do you really mean it?"

"Sure thing," Black Dog said, then looked at Tom. "Sorry, but there's no gift for you."

"Then could you give me some answers?"

"What's on your mind?"

"Well, to tell the truth, I always suspected you were the person behind all the strange events at Lunenburg Manor. If you weren't pulling off a crime, what *were* you doing?"

Black Dog laughed, and squeezed Tom's shoulder with a hand that was surprisingly powerful. "Appearances are deceptive, Tom. Just because I have a black beard doesn't mean I'm Blackbeard, or some other villain. I'm just another artist, struggling to succeed."

"But what about that morning we met you at the cove, near the Ovens? When we told you the Professor was dead, you shouted *the fools—I warned them!* and went running off. How come?"

"It was the police I was upset about, because I thought they'd let the Professor be murdered despite my warnings. Do you remember visiting the school, and saying the Zincks were in danger?"

"Sure."

"I was already worried about them, so your suspicions forced me to act. After you left the school, I went to the police station and warned them to watch Henneyberry. But they didn't take me seriously, because everyone in town knows that I've been feuding with Henneyberry for years."

"Why?"

Black Dog laughed. "I've never met anyone so fond of asking questions! Anyway, to continue, I was talking to Cap'n John one day and he mentioned that Henneyberry had asked if his tour boat could stand up to heavy seas."

"I guess so he could put the Zincks overboard off the Ovens, during a storm."

"From then on I used my telescope to keep an eye on the tour boat. Unfortunately, I was in Halifax when the storm struck, but I got back just in time to spot Henneyberry taking you kids and

Professor Zinck out to the boat. I alerted the police, then drove to the cliff above the Ovens to watch for the boat coming out from Lunenburg."

"Did you see it?"

"Yes, but there was no sign of a police boat in pursuit. I started to panic, because I knew Henneyberry was up to something terrible. So I ran to the cove, grabbed one of the motorboats that I rent when I'm scuba-diving, and headed out to sea."

"Wearing your black scuba-diving suit for warmth?"

Black Dog nodded. "I could see the lights of the tour boat through the storm, but my motorboat couldn't catch up. Then, for some reason, the tour boat stopped moving and I was able to get close to it."

"That's when Liz killed the engine, and forced Henneyberry to throw his gun overboard."

"By the time the tour boat was going again, I was right alongside. I grabbed the rope at the bow, managed to make my boat fast, and then struggled on board. I crawled along the cabin roof, saw what was happening, and made my leap at Henneyberry."

"Superman to the rescue!" Tom said, laughing. "You sure had everything under control by the time the police boat reached us and arrested Henneyberry."

Liz looked at Black Dog. "How'd you get so strong? Was it from scuba-diving?"

"That's right. I started diving to build up my muscles, then got hooked on it. You kids should try it some time. If you like adventure and mystery, there's no detective work like searching for wrecks and their treasures."

"Sign me up!" Tom said. "Say, I guess that explains why you were at the cove that morning. You'd been scuba-diving."

"And that's where I'm going now." Black Dog waved. "Before you leave Lunenburg, be sure to drop by the school to say goodbye."

Liz gazed after Black Dog until he was lost from sight. "There goes the greatest man I'll ever know," she said wistfully.

Tom laughed. "What about Cap'n John? You seemed to think he was pretty great, too."

Liz's face lit up. "Do you suppose he's here?"

"Maybe he's in that building with the displays of fancy equipment for tracking fish. Want to go see?"

"O.K., but what about the Ox Pull? I don't want to miss that, or the Queen of the Sea contest. Not to mention a few more rides on the *Tilt-A-Whirl*."

They headed toward a large crowd which had gathered for the Ox Pull. Standing with the Zincks watching the event were Carl and Shirley, who smiled in greeting.

"The Ox Pull is a big attraction at Maritime exhibitions," Shirley said. "This is total muscle power!"

"Is it like a tug-of-war?"

Carl shook his head. "You see that team of oxen? They're about to be hitched to a cart with a dead weight of over three thousand kilos. If the team can manage to shift the cart forward, it will win the contest."

111

The smooth brown coats of the two enormous beasts shimmered and rippled as they were led into place. Brass bells clanged at their throats as they shook their great heads and prepared for the challenge. The teamster, standing before them, reached a hand to one of their curved horns and then shouted a command. The animals dug their feet in, the wood of their yoke groaned, and the cart moved slowly forward to loud applause from the audience.

"How are you feeling?" Tom asked the Zincks.

"Fully recovered," Mrs. Zinck said, smiling. "I found out I was ill because Henneyberry was putting something in my food, to keep me out of action. After the murder he increased the dose, so I was too feeble to go for help."

"I knew it, Liz! Didn't I say he was poisoning the food?"

"I have to admit you got that one."

Tom looked at the Professor. "And now I know why you wrote EVEL in the dirt."

"I was attacked at the Money Pit by Henneyberry and my brother, who rushed into hiding when they heard you two coming. I was too weak to get away, so I tried to write the names of my attackers in the dirt. Unfortunately I passed out after writing the first letters of Evelyn's name."

Tom shook his head. "I should have figured that out, especially since I knew your twin brother had a girl's name."

Liz nodded. "And we'd even discussed adult twins, that day in the cemetery."

"Oh well. You can't win them all!"

Liz grew thoughtful. "So I guess that forerunner that you told us about was really your brother?"

The Professor nodded sadly. "At the time I thought the vision had been of myself, but it was my twin who was doomed."

The group headed toward a building which throbbed with the amplified music of a hillbilly band. Liz imitated the wild motions of a berserk fiddle player, then grinned at the Zincks.

"I love those country sounds! Say, Professor Zinck, did you hear that Tom swore he saw your ghost? Talk about running scared!"

"It's true!" Tom exclaimed. "I'm sure you were at the tower window, during the storm."

"You're right, Tom. I'd broken free of the ropes that Henneyberry had tied me up with, and started shouting for help when I couldn't get the window open. Then Henneyberry rushed into the room, and put me out with a gas capsule."

"Visiting the Manor always freaked me. Those creaky floors, and the time when Evelyn had secretly taken your place and was acting so strangely. He was muttering about life and death, I guess because he couldn't stand the thought of murder."

"Poor Evelyn."

Liz was now nimbly plucking an invisible banjo. "I'll tell you a clue we missed. It happened when we returned your car keys after finding them at Oak Island."

"Car keys? But I don't drive."

"Exactly! They must have actually been your house keys, but Evelyn just said that he was in no shape to drive, and gave the keys to Henneyberry.

We should have known that your place had been taken by an imposter, who didn't know that you don't drive. It also showed that Henneyberry was involved, because he didn't say anything about Evelyn's mistake."

Inside the building, a mob of people was packed around a stage which shook and quivered with the electronic vibrations of the music. The soaring beauty of a fiddle carried a song to its close, and the crowd cheered wildly.

Suddenly, a pirate leapt onto the stage. As his cutlass flashed, the band cowered back and the audience gasped. Then Roger Eliot-Stanton hurried from the wings and approached the microphone.

"Ladies and gentlemen!" he said, holding up his hands for quiet. "Thank you for participating in a small experiment. Your fear of this pirate shows that I have selected the right person to play Captain Kidd in my next movie."

Excited chattering broke out, then died away when the pirate made threatening gestures with his cutlass. Roger Eliot-Stanton motioned the pirate to his side. "My friends!" he cried. "May I present the silver screen's next superstar!"

With a flourish, he pulled away the pirate's eyepatch and false beard. For a moment the crowd was shocked into silence, then wild whistles and cheers broke out as Cap'n John grinned and waved his cutlass in the air. When the noise finally ended, the band returned to its playing and the two men came down from the stage.

Tom and Liz pushed forward among the crush of locals to congratulate Cap'n John on becoming a celebrity. Hoping to question Roger Eliot-Stanton, Tom elbowed a path to his side.

"Are you a real movie director?"

"Yes."

"Are you actually going to make a movie about Captain Kidd?"

"Yes."

"Will you be filming at Oak Island?"

"Yes."

"Is Cap'n John really going to star?"

"Yes."

"Are you looking for a second star?"

"No."

Obviously the man had no eye for talent, and Tom lost interest in asking questions. But Liz wanted some answers, too.

"How'd you meet Cap'n John?"

"I chartered his boat to do some location scouting. As soon as I saw him, I knew that the great Eliot-Stanton had made another fabulous discovery."

"You were at Lunenburg Manor once, saying the Professor could name his own price for something. What did you want?"

Roger Eliot-Stanton smiled, and his face came close to looking pleasant. "Thanks for the reminder, young lady. I'd forgotten about that unfinished business."

"But what did you want?"

"The Manor would be a perfect location for some scenes in my movie." Sliding close to the Zincks, Roger Eliot-Stanton allowed his smile to grow wider. "Perhaps you'd agree to my company using the Manor? I would pay you handsomely."

115

Professor Zinck laughed. "The money doesn't matter. You can have the Manor for free, but there's one condition."

"What's that?"

The Professor nodded toward Tom and Liz. "I have two good friends who would love to do some acting. Do you suppose you could find them something in your movie?"

Roger Eliot-Stanton's smile faded. Then he wrapped his arms around Tom and Liz. "Of course! These kids are my buddies! There's nothing I wouldn't do for them."

Wriggling free of the bony arm, Tom looked at Professor Zinck. "Thanks a million, Professor! I hope that both of you will visit us at our Hollywood mansion."

Mrs. Zinck laughed. "We'll be there for sure."

\* \* \*

Later that night, a silver moon looked down on two figures who moved silently through the black forest. Somewhere in the darkness an owl hooted, and a small creature rustled through the underbrush, but these sounds were ignored by Wade and Tom as they followed the faint outline of the path leading to Phantom Cove.

The two were after buried treasure. As everyone knows, such treasure can only be dug for at night, and in total silence. But there was another legend that both boys could not help thinking about: *If blood was shed by pirates burying their booty, then it must also flow before the gold and jewels can be dug up.*

Tom shivered, imagining the terrible eyes of the spectral pirate who might be guarding the treasure at Phantom Cove. He glanced at Wade, wondering how brave his companion felt.

A moan came from somewhere in the night.

Wade's steps faltered, but Tom pushed bravely forward. For a moment it seemed he would have to go on alone. Then Wade hurried to his side and they continued their silent journey.

Again they heard the moan, a fearful sound that grew louder and louder until it filled their ears.

Then they saw it.

On the path directly ahead stood a headless body, wearing a white suit that seemed smudged with the dirt of the grave. Moonlight shone on the horrible creature as it slowly raised its arms, moaning.

Wade screamed. The shriek of terror vibrated in his throat, filling the air. *"Help! Murder!"* he cried, then broke into a swift run and was gone. For several minutes his screams were heard, fading away into the night, and then all was silence.

Except for Tom's laughter, which went on for a long time. He turned to the headless body with a grin. "That's the last time Wade will reach through my bedroom window with icy fingers. Revenge is sweet."

There was a muffled reply, then Liz pulled away the black velvet that had covered her head. "What fun!" she said. "One night soon I'm going to try haunting someone else. I wonder where I could find a nice juicy victim?"

"Don't even think about it!"

Liz laughed wickedly. "I can't wait, dear brother."